DAY ONE

VOLUME 1 OF THE KACHADA SERIES

DAY

:Birth is a death sentence

ONE

DON SEDEI

The Amusement Park, LLC

This book is a work of fiction. The names, characters and events in this book are the products of the author's imagination or are used fictitiously. Any similarity to real persons living or dead is coincidental and not intended by the author.

DAY ONE: Birth is a death sentence,
Volume 1 of the Kachada Series

Published by The Amusement Park, LLC

Cover designed and illustrated by Don Sedei

ISBN (hardcover): 9781642370706
ISBN (paperback): 9781642372816
eISBN: 9781642372823
LCCN: 2018951819

Printed in the United States of America

CONTENTS

DEDICATIONS

Joanne
My beautiful wife for supporting and encouraging me to be a dream chaser

Richard and David
My two amazing sons

Jennifer
My hero and Daddy's little girl

Mia and Ellie
Our Great Pyrenees and Papillon who patiently sat by my side waiting to be petted

Sammie
The elusive cat who hates to be petted

ACKNOWLEDGMENTS

Every novel presents its own unique set of challenges, and this novel series is no different. As always, there are those who inspired me and supported my journey to help make this dream come true.

John—The brave and brilliant man who inspired the Kachada Series.

My siblings—Robert, Karol, Ken, and Diane

My La Roche College roommates and alumni—David and Mary Ann Nicholls, Dave and Cindy Saxon Getty, Tony Czadankiewicz and Gary Watson

My Albuquerque neighbors—Tom and Diana McEnnerney

My editors—Alexandra, Cassandra, Jessica, Tahlia, Wendy, and Gatekeeper Press

My special thanks to—My loyal friend and talented business partner Ross Myers

And to my longtime friend—Stan Muschweck, *The Wizard*, a brilliant man and the main protagonist in my upcoming novel to be released sometime in the near future, *Tale of Bronco & The Wizard*, a light-hearted urban fantasy about football and wizards.

ONCE YOU TURN THIS PAGE...

...you will enter the unimaginable journey of Kachada Toscano where the unlikely tale of two parallel universes—the chilling ancestral traditions of the Comanche Tribe and the ruthless code of the Sicilian Mafia—mysteriously intersect. His impassioned narrative uncovers a precarious future and the riddles of a malevolent past that will reside on the backside of your eyelids, causing many a restless night.

CHAPTER 1

March 27, 1954, 3:15 a.m.
Pittsburgh Medical Center

"Kachada is your name: Remember, birth is a death sentence. So make every minute count." Those were the first words my mother whispered into my ear at birth as I embarked on this existential journey into a cognate world of mystery and chaos.

From the beginning, I was both blessed and cursed with a photographic memory. The first images I recall were two masked faces holding me down. The only time in my life I felt outnumbered.

I was born Kachada Toscano to Taabe Peta who was married to Antonio Toscano.

I was given the Comanche name Kachada, meaning "white man," by my mother, a brilliant scientist who worked alongside Doctor Jonas Salk. She was a full-blooded Comanche and the daughter of the leader of the *Lord of The Plains,* Comanche Chief Peta. My father served in the Second World War with the Office of Strategic Services (OSS) as an officer collecting intelligence in France. This group was the predecessor of the modern Central Intelligence Agency (CIA). He was the only surviving son of Giovanni Toscano, The Godfather of Franklin, Pennsylvania's Sicilian Mafia. It was this ancestry that provided me with the courage to survive.

CHAPTER 2

August 27, 1988, Alexandria, Virginia

Blackness surrounds me. Unable to see any distinguishable shapes or colors, I lean against the doorway. Eerie, unnerving sounds of bedlam fill the air—doors slamming, struggling and quick breaths of anxiety. I try to calm myself to keep my heartbeat steady in spite of the rising chaos.

A flash of blue light reveals a silhouette running down a stairway. Others chase after it. The footsteps stop, then quickly move again throughout the three floors of the mansion.

Sounds coming from several different areas are getting closer. I remain quiet, barely moving out of the moonlight. The door opens, so I step into the black background like a chameleon. Where'd they come from? How many are out there? The door closes. The mystery person moves on.

My mind whirls. *Fight or flight?*

Running from danger has never been a natural response for me. I can think my way out of most situations. I hear the sounds of footsteps going from room to room, opening doors, looking for me.

I knew he would be a difficult mark, but I didn't think I would eventually become the prey. I rotate my head to pick up the faintest sound, or vibration within the mansion. Scanning the perimeter of the black room, I recognize the unmistakable click of the beveled steel chamber of a Sterling MKB 9mm.

Some people are blessed with an ear for music. I have an ear for high-powered weapons. Now the shroud of mystery is lifted—that click tells me I'm up against an elite group.

He set me up, left a false trail to his summer home. Time to make a decision to escape or be trapped, with the task of eliminating everyone but my target. I review the floor plan in my head: a typical Old Virginia mansion. Depending on the period and architect, there could be twelve to fifteen rooms, excluding the basement and maid's quarters. Footsteps draw closer. Too close. I explode out of blackness and *kick open* the door, knocking down one of the stalkers. Straddling the guy, I bury a 9mm bullet into his forehead. *I realized I just shot Max.*

I've killed many who deserved it, but *Max*, the Marine Corps Forces Special Operations Command, assigned as Director Nicholls' right-hand man, was not one of them. This world I'm caught up in provides its share of ugly regrets.

A flurry of bullets descends on me, tracking my movements as I race to the stairs. Steady streams of drywall, plaster, and glass fragments shower me as I bolt down the long narrow corridor. To keep a low target profile, I slide down the stairs on my side rather than run.

I make my way through the mansion. Continuous gunfire rips apart the rooms behind me. In thirty seconds, I reach the back door, finding it ajar. I squeeze through it, only to be startled by a black cat running past me. *Not exactly a good omen.* Voices and footsteps ring out as I make a beeline for the dark silhouette of the Patrick Henry Woods.

Nestled up against a chestnut tree a few rows deep, with a clear full-moon view of the house, I brace for an unwelcome introduction. No one comes. I'm not sure why. The only sounds are a swinging porch door, a far-off wind chime and disgruntled voices. *I can't believe I killed Max.*

Nicholls set me up. He's proven to be a clever and powerful man, and now I have to start my search for him all over again, as difficult as it is. Because of him I've been torturing myself with the memories of my covert partner, Joanne, the faces of Nisar's wife and children, blacking out and going into my Comanche rage. If only I had been able to control myself . . . all those years of guilt.

I make an about-face and limp deeper into the woods as my right leg is going numb. I heard again my mother's haunting words, *"Kachada: Remember, birth is a death sentence. So make every minute count."* I stop to reach into my pocket and sniff the cocaine-laced nasal spray I call my best friend. It helps with the pain and gives me the courage to teeter on that razor-thin edge. The price I pay for still being alive—7,051,800 minutes longer than anyone expected.

CHAPTER 3

Day One, July 17, 2010, Vernon, Texas

My radio is blasting "Not Afraid", by Eminem, three miles down a paved road off the Chisholm Trail Parkway. I drive up to a red brick mansion surrounded by timber fences keeping the longhorn steers and mustangs separated. A cowboy valet asks for my keys and drives off with my Viper.

"Mr. Toscano. Welcome to the Thorn Ranch. I'm Jon, the Senator's personal aid," a tall young man wearing khaki Dockers and a powder blue V-neck sweater said politely.

"How long have they been here?" I ask, pointing to a helicopter marked United States of America in a cleared pasture with two Marines standing guard.

"They arrived thirty minutes ago. Anxious to meet you," Jon said.

"I'll bet they are. Is that John with an *H*?" I ask.

"No sir, Jonathon. Jonathon Alan."

"A man with two first names. You must be an Ivy leaguer."

"Princeton 2004. Please follow me sir." I follow Jon through the long hallway filled with western paintings and sculptures by the likes of "Charles Marion Russell and Frederic Remington" into an even larger room. "Can I get you something to drink?" Jon asks.

I am in awe of the art. "No thanks."

"Please make yourself at home. I will let the senator know you're here." Jon leaves the room.

I wander into another room admiring the cowhide-covered chairs, the majestic stone fireplace with lariats, rifles and pistols hanging on the walls among the Terpning, Dixon and Johnson paintings of the Wild West. They remind me of my grandfather's paintings. In the middle of the room sits a green felt pool table with the lone star burned into the leather pockets. Just what I would imagine a Texas oil baron's mansion should look like. Jon returns from behind a herd of longhorn steers carved into the tall wood doors.

"Mr. Toscano, please follow me." Jon asks.

I say, "Give me a moment."

"Yes sir." Jon said politely.

I ask myself. *Do I really want to go through with this?* Thanks to the pressures of social media and fiction written about me it's time the truth be told.

I follow Jon through the massive wood carved doors and into a room of high ceilings, burgundy painted walls, wood beams, and iron images of longhorn steers making up the oversized chandelier above an eighteen-foot long solid wood table. The brown leather chairs have the ranch's brand burned into the headdress. Silver platters line the table with tacos, burritos and all the Tex-Mex condiments. The American Flag and Texas Flag are framed and hung facing each other hanging on opposite walls among historical pictures of the family and ranch.

It's my first appearance in public since the blurred image of my 1976 CIA mug shot. A digital copy of a copy some blogger posted on his site. Six pairs of serious looking eyes follow me as I am escorted to my seat at the table. Since my right leg has become less mobile I pull it along as I walk, making for an awkward entry.

A tall gray-haired Texan says, "Mr. Toscano, thank you for coming." I set my six hundred ninety-five dollar Zero Halliburton attaché on the table. My life is filled with details about anything important to me. I look up and notice Senator Cornwall's befuddled expression.

"Augusto had blonde hair and Caesar had blue eyes. The Germans and the Celtic people influenced the Roman Empire as well as the Toscano ancestry." I said.

"Mr. Toscano, I believe I speak for all of my fellow senators when I say thank you for meeting with us today. I am Senator John Cornwall from Texas, Chairman of The U.S.

Senate Select Committee on Intelligence. Let me introduce my colleagues, Senators Richard Boon from North Carolina, James Rouch from Idaho, Jose Rubin from Florida, Sissy Wyatt from Maine and Brice Linkletter from Oklahoma. Before we start, is there anything I can do to make you comfortable?" Senator Cornwall asks.

I have to laugh and say, "Huh, being here makes me uncomfortable, Mr. Chairman." I struggle to pull my leg under the table and move my attaché to the right of me.

Senator Rubin interjects, "Please, take all the time you need."

"Yes, the one thing I can never count on Senator is time." I open and reach into my attaché, taking out my tech toys, cell phone, mini laptop and say, "I love this." I hold up my Swiss Army Knife. "It has 87 implements and 1412 functions. I admire the details of superior craftsmanship."

Senator Cornwall asks, "Can we get you anything? Coffee, ice tea, water?"

I glance up from my toys. "A bottle of 50-year-old Mac 'M' scotch."

"Sir?" Senator Cornwall's face turns stupid.

"That's what I would like," I ask, to see how far they will go to accommodate me.

"I'll send Jon to hunt that down. Would a cup of coffee do for now?" Asks Senator Cornwall.

I say, "Yes. No cream. No sugar. In an eight-ounce ceramic white cup, and no logos on the cup, please. I hate advertising on cups." My idiosyncrasies show.

Jon runs out with a pitcher of ice water and a glass, setting it to my right. "Is it okay if I put this here, sir?" Jon asks.

I figure I'd give him an Attaboy. "Thanks, Jon." I reach into my attaché and take out my rosary beads, uncurling them in my palm.

Senator Wyatt lifts her chin to get a better view says, "The rosary. I've read you always carry them with you."

Holding them up, I point to the flawless detail of the craftsmanship. "My grandfather, Chief Peta, hand-carved each rosary bead, telling a story of my ancestors."

"The split feather?" asks Senator Linkletter.

"A symbol for a wounded warrior. The silver feather represents my Comanche ancestry, the ruby and emerald beads represent my Sicilian ancestry."

Senator Linkletter asks, "Wounded?"

I reply, "My diagnosis."

"Yes, one of the few notes I could read in your dossier. What would you prefer I call you? Kachada or JT?"

"Mr. Toscano or sir," I said.

"Mr. Toscano it is," Said Senator Cornwall. "Before we begin I will need to swear you in before this committee under oath. It's a matter of procedure. You may stay seated if you wish Mr. Toscano. Raise your right hand?"

I pull my leg from under the table to stand and say, "Nothing will keep me from standing up for my country, Senator."

"Do you solemnly swear to tell the truth the whole truth and nothing but the truth so help you God?" asks Senator Rouch.

I pause to look directly at each Senator. I can see each of their perplexed faces, confused by my hesitation, and say, "I do."

"Thank you Mr. Toscano, please be seated and relax," says Senator Rouch. I struggle to return to the seated position.

"As you know Mr. Toscano this an informal meeting, not a hearing. Which is why the other members of this committee are not here with us today. This is a fact-finding mission to clarify the stories and rumors of your alleged covert activities connected to the Department of Defense from the years of 1975 to 2002. I'm sure you have read the blogs on the Internet," says Senator Rubin.

"You mean that fiction bullshit? Yes," I reply.

Senator Wyatt says, "Yes, well Mr. Toscano. Your file is a mystery. A mystery we gathered here to find answers to. In front of us is a dossier that has been passed on to us from previous administrations. It listed covert CIA missions assigned by Directors Robert Panos and Stewart Nicholls. None of which are documented as Directors of the CIA. Your name was attached to them. The file is filled with blacked-out pages, leaving us incomplete notes dating from December 1975 through

2002. Which is why we were asked by the Secretary of Defense to uncover what is under those blacked out pages."

"The truth, Senator Wyatt, is blacker than those pages you have in front of you," I reply.

Senator Boon says, "Mr. Toscano," We have been given authority to provide you with complete immunity if you cooperate with us on clearing up the mysteries in this dossier."

After a short pause I say, "Senators, if I reveal what you cannot see, I need the President's signature on that immunity. I don't want to live out what time I have left in Guantanamo Bay."

Senator Cornwall says, "Yes, well Mr. Toscano we are aware of your meticulous need for details and knew you might ask." Senator Boon passes me the signed document.

I read the document to make sure I'm not being set up and say. "My apologies Senators, but I've learned to never trust anyone, especially the government."

Senator Cornwall says, "Well, sir, as the Chairman of this committee I promise you can trust us. We have no agenda here other than finding the truth."

Senator Boon adds, "That being said, we only have two days. So, if I may, let me start with a mysterious covert operation identified as Propaganda."

Senator Wyatt says, "We have reason to believe it was set up as a secret arm of the CIA."

"An ingenious and very successful one," I reply.

Senator Linkletter asks, "So it's true?"

Looking at every senator I say, "Senators, everything I tell you during these next two days is true."

Senator Boon says, "Which is why you are here. To help us find that truth."

"Senator, the truth is ugly." They glance at each other. "Are you sure you want to know?" I ask.

The only sound you can hear is my ice cubes melting in my water glass. Senator Linkletter breaks the silence and says, "Mr. Toscano, I have an article in front of me written twenty-two years ago by the *Washington*

Post about an E-5, Sergeant Joseph Maxmillian Mayer, who was killed in Alexandria, Virginia. Your name has surfaced in a blog as the one responsible for killing this marine."

Hearing Max's full name for the very first time caused my heart to skip a beat. "Joseph Maxmillian Mayer?" I muttered.

"Sorry, I couldn't hear. What did you say, Mr. Toscano?" Senator Wyatt asks.

I hear the Senator but my mind has wandered off. *I can only see the blonde fair-skinned Max standing outside Director Pano's office in his Marine desert-sand Cammies.*

"Mr. Toscano? Could you please answer Senator Wyatt's question?" Senator Rubin asks.

I look up and say, "Yes."

"Yes what, Mr. Toscano?" asks Senator Boon.

Without hesitation I reply, "Yes, I killed Max."

Senator Rubin says, "Mr. Toscano, are you admitting to killing a United States Marine? That could mean death by firing squad."

I remind them and say, "Senator, I have total immunity."

Senator Rouch asks, “The story written in the blog is true then?”

“No. No, I read the blog and it is not accurate. Yes, I regret killing Max. But I’m not remorseful.” I stop for only a moment and say, “I was trapped in the dark and had no idea Max was the one chasing me. Director Nicholls had me lured to his mansion to have me killed.”

Senator Boon asks, “Why would this Mr. Nicholls want to kill you?”

“I found out he was responsible for the faces that haunt me at night,” I reply.

Senator Linkletter asks, “Haunt you? What faces?”

“The ones he led me to believe I killed.”

“Killed?” Senator Boon asks.

Senator Wyatt says, “Mr. Toscano, Do we have your approval to record this conversation?”

Senator Cornwall interrupts, “Senator Boon and my fellow committee members, I have a request.”

Senator Rouch asks, “Mr. Chairman?”

"I would like to break from the traditional format here. We have all been in countless meetings with a dossier that has words, sentences and paragraphs blacked out, but I have never been handed a dossier where pages upon pages of the information in it has been blacked out. Have any of you?" Senator Cornwall asks.

Senator Rouch replies, "No, Mr. Chairman." The other senators all nod in agreement.

"I thought as much," says Senator Cornwall. He turns to me and says, "Mr. Toscano I have a simple request. Unusual, but a simple one you can ignore if you wish. The only overview given to my fellow senators on this committee and me says you have a photographic memory; you speak eight languages other than English. They list them as Italian, French, Hebrew, Spanish, German, Russian, Arabic and, the one that caught my eye, Comanche. It goes on to say you have varying degrees of black belts in all the martial arts. That doesn't surprise me considering the world you have been living in. That's all we have about you other than a vague note about a cancer diagnosis. We have no information on where you were born, what your background is. Nothing that gives us any insight on what brought you to such a dark place. I plan on retiring after this year Mr. Toscano. And through all of the official committee hearings, of which this one is not, I have always wanted to ask this question."

"Senator?" I ask.

"If my fellow senators agree," the Senator acknowledges his fellow committee members. "I would like to know how these pages of black became your life. In other words Mr. Toscano I want to, or would like to know, sir, how the hell did Kachada become this supposed assassin, or should I say, a silent warrior for our country?"

Senator Linkletter blurts out, "Senators. Is this really necessary? We only have two days with Mr. Toscano. We owe it this committee to keep on task."

Senator Boon says, "I agree. I want to get to the meat of this. No offense Mr. Toscano, but I don't give a shit how you got to be an assassin or this silent warrior. I just want to know how, why and who gave you the orders to kill."

"Let it be recorded that Senator Boon and Senator Linkletter have voiced their concerns," Senator Cornwall says.

Senator Rouch chirps in, "I agree with the Chairman and my fellow Senator Cornwall. I am also curious and would like to know what these blacked out pages don't have beneath them."

Senators Rubin speaks up. "I'm in agreement with Senator Rouch."

"I do as well," says Senator Wyatt.

Senator Cornwall says, "Mr. Toscano. Let me remind you, this is not an official hearing. You have the freedom to get up and leave and not answer any of our questions whenever you wish. But this is the opportunity, Mr. Toscano, to present us with the truth of your story."

Looking at the Senators argue, I began to think. *The truth is why I am here. There is no one left for it to harm.* "Senators."

"Yes, Mr. Toscano?" Senator Wyatt asks.

"Senators, where would you like me to begin?" I ask.

"I am curious about you and what I have heard Mr. Toscano. Personally, I would like to hear your story from the very beginning. If my fellow members agree." Senator Rubin says.

Senators Wyatt, Cornwall and Rouch nod yes. Senators Boon and Linkletter shake their heads no. Senator Cornwall says, "Four to two. Mr. Toscano, you may start at the beginning."

"I want all of this recorded. Everything I say here during the next two days is, as I swore earlier, nothing but the truth. I want the halls of the Senate, Congress and White House to know I have no remorse for killing those who deserved to be killed," I say.

Silence came over the room. Senator Cornwall says, "Senator Rouch, please let it be noted that Mr. Toscano asked we record everything he says during these next two days."

Senator Wyatt says, "Mr. Toscano, it is day one and the room is yours."

I pour water into my glass and hold it up. "What do you see, Senators?" Senator Cornwall's face looks perplexed. I ask again, "What do you see?"

Senator Rubin's face turns pink, not knowing what to say. "Half full or half empty, depending on your point of view."

I set my glass down, "That, Senators, is shrink bullshit. Half full or half empty is a fucking political cop-out. This is how I live my life, Senators. The Comanche believe the land is your spirit. You live within it; you don't piss on it. In other words, the amount of water in this glass is all I need to survive. Never wasting what nature gives you."

I take a sip from the water glass and say, "For the record Senators, as a young man I had dreams of becoming a neurosurgeon. I dreamed of saving lives, not taking them." I pause and begin to reflect saying, "But I learned early on, my life was destined to be anything but normal."

CHAPTER 4

March 28, 1959,
Franklin, Pennsylvania

Up to the age of five my life was normal. Then it wasn't.

"Kachada. Kachada. Wake up."

I rubbed my eyes. "Mom, what?

Her face was wet from crying. "You father, Kachada. He died of a heart attack." No hug. No kiss of sympathy.

"I don't understand," I said.

Then she whispered, *"Trust no one, Kachada. Not even your mother."* And left my room.

I couldn't stop crying. It was one day after my fifth birthday. My dad surrounded me. My dresser tops and walls were filled with photos of Dad and me. He loved baseball. We loved baseball. On my fourth birthday he gave me a signed Roberto Clemente poster to hang on the back of my door. My cigar box filled with baseball cards sat on my nightstand. Dad and I spent hours flipping those cards.

All of a sudden, I heard voices arguing downstairs catching my attention. I walked to the railing and saw mom standing next to two men in military uniforms, having a heated discussion. I couldn't make out what they were saying except when they mentioned my name. Frightened, I returned to my room and cried myself to sleep.

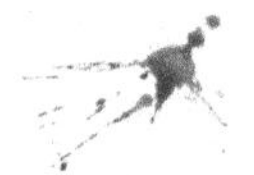

"Kachada, time to go." It was morning and Mom was backlit from early sunrise coming through my window. She held my dad's duffle bag, packed and ready to go.

My eyes were dry from crying all night. "Mom? Where are we going?' I asked.

She didn't say and hustled me to Dad's car. We drove for two days, stopping three times for gas and once for breakfast at Stucky's. I finally mustered up the courage and asked again, "Mom, where are we going?"

"I'm taking you to live with my father, your grandpa," Mom said.

"What? Why? I don't want to leave you," I pleaded.

"Kachada, you will love grandpa."

"Grandpa? I don't know him," I said.

Mom said, "He'll teach you how to survive in this dangerous world."

"Survive? Dangerous? I don't understand."

"We'll be there in a few hours," Mom said.

I stared out the car window, watching snow-covered roads becoming clear, sunny highways. We turned off at exit 37 onto a dirt road. We drove about two miles or so down that dirt road to a sign, "Welcome To The Comanche Nation. Lords Of The Plains." We continued on to a cluster of wood and stone homes.

"Mom, I don't like this place. It's dirty," I said.

Mom stopped at a small, multi-colored wood-framed home. A larger-than-life man, wearing a feathered headdress and buckskin stood in front of the house. He spoke an odd language to my mother as she gathered my duffle bag and handed it to me. She kneeled down. "Kachada, this is your grandpa, my father, Comanche Chief Peta. Today is your first day of becoming a Comanche warrior." I had no idea what that meant, standing in front of her on that hot dusty day. She abruptly got up and said, "I will return," And drove off in Dad's green Plymouth Belvedere.

Here I was, a young boy from Franklin, Pennsylvania, left standing next to this smelly wrinkled man in a colorful shirt and a long feathered headdress. He put his heavy hands on my shoulders, taking my duffle bag, and started to walk away, speaking English: "We only speak Comanche here. I will teach you," he said.

I was still fixated on the dust rising from my mother driving in the distance. In four days my life as I knew it was over. My father was gone, and my mother was driving away, leaving me in this world of dust, dirt, and red skinned faces speaking a strange language. I knew now that my life was destined to be anything but normal.

The next morning I sat cross-legged in a half circle on a dirt floor, wearing buckskin. Chief Peta spoke English, so I could understand, telling us about the Comanche ancestors. He said, *'Your ancestry has everything to do with your future.'* As he spoke I looked around at the other young braves listening to his every word. They looked nothing like me. The Chief went on to describe a brutal bloody scene about a Comanche raid. Comanche Chief Quanah, my great-grandfather, I later learned, was the fierce warrior leading the raid on a Pawnee village in return for stealing Comanche horses. Chief Peta taught us how the Comanche warriors left every Pawnee brave, woman and child either tortured or dead. It was horrifying listening to the details of it. He ended the long story with a Comanche legacy: *'Leave no enemy alive. They will only return to kill us all.'* A legacy that would return to haunt me.

I arrived as a five-year-old white boy having no idea how much I would learn to love my Comanche ancestry and the Comanche life.

I was ten years old riding my spotted pony next to Chief Peta. He was a wise man teaching me to become a warrior and how to survive and live as one with the land. Every day since I arrived was a new adventure, learning about the Comanche and the history of my ancestors. I listened to his lesson for the day. He said, *"Kachada, to survive in the beauty of nature you have to kill the ugly beasts that live within it."*

I asked him, "What ugly beasts?"

He smiled and said, "You will know them when you meet them."

Before I could ask what he meant, he stopped my pony, watching a trail of dust rise in the distance. Then Chief Peta gave me the nod to ride on. Together we rode up to my mother who was standing next to her green Belvedere. She was wearing her white lab coat and blue hospital attire. This was the first I had seen of my mother since the day she left me on the reservation five years ago. She looked happier than the day she brought me. Her long silky black hair was blowing in the wind, reminding me just how beautiful she was, this tall slender woman who carried the poise and dignity of a true Comanche. It was a treat to see her smile. The Chief and I climbed off our horses. I stood in front of her, very proper, listening to Grandpa and Mom speak.

"You are back as you promised," Chief Peta said.

"Yes, Dad," Mom said respectfully.

The Chief spoke firmly, "He is a Comanche warrior now. Just as you wished."

"He looks so strong and beautiful."

The Chief put his hand on my shoulder. "His Comanche spirit is forever part of him now."

"I am here to keep my promise to Antonio," Mom said.

When she mentioned Dad's name it gave me the chills. She kneeled down. "Kachada, now you and I must return to Franklin."

"Why?" I asked.

Chief Peta put his heavy hand back on my shoulder, reminding me to be quiet. He walked into his weathered post-war home. The house was set on concrete blocks with a covered stoop, which created a home for a metal glider painted tar black and covered with an Indian blanket any art collector would love to have. He returned through the screen door carrying the same duffle bag I came with. When I arrived, the Chief took it from me. I had lived in buckskin and moccasins every day since. Now he handed me the duffle bag. I glanced at him and obediently followed Mom to the car. I never took my eyes off the Chief. I held my bag as I rolled down the car window, watching him disappear into the dust from the tires of mom's Belvedere. I was leaving what had become my home, the legacy of my Comanche ancestors, as a warrior wondering: *What would become of me?*

"I fail to see what this has to do with the reason of this hearing," Senator Boon complains.

Senator Cornwall replies, "Senator Boon. Let me remind you, this is an unofficial meeting. Not a hearing. The normal proceedings don't apply. You have no obligation to stay. No one here would condemn you if you chose to leave. Perhaps you would rather be on the golf course?"

Senator Boon says, "Senator Cornwall and my fellow committee members, I excuse myself. Sorry, I mean no disrespect, Mr. Toscano. Have a good day." He slams his briefcase shut as Jon shows him out of the room.

Senator Cornwall asks, "If anyone else here would like excuse themselves, please feel free to leave." He looks around the table and gets the nod to proceed. "Please continue, Mr. Toscano. I promise there will be no more interruptions."

"Senator. Has the scotch arrived?" I ask.

Senator Cornwall asks, "Jon, any news on Mr. Toscano's scotch?" Jon walks quickly to Senator Cornwall and whispers something. "Mr. Toscano. Your scotch should be here shortly," Senator Cornwall says.

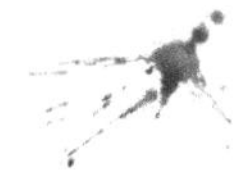

CHAPTER 5

March 31, 1964, Lawton, Oklahoma

During the long ride from the reservation, Mom took my buckskin clothes and moccasins and placed them in my duffle bag. She gave me jeans, a t-shirt, sneakers and a plaid shirt to change into. We drove up to the massive front porch I remembered: a large craftsman style wooden house, surrounded by oversized maple trees. A cluster of people had gathered, and among them were two faces I recognized. Grandpa Giovanni standing next to Grandma Isabel. They opened the car door, took me and passed me from one big hug and wet kiss to another. The feeling of being hugged and kissed was new to me. So different than when I arrived at the Reservation, looking up at the solemn face of the Chief I learned to love.

My Sicilian grandparents were successful business people and powerful members of the community. They whisked my mother and me into the big house to a long wooden table filled with food and new smells. There were so many kinds of bread, pasta, and meats waiting for us. We ate until we couldn't breathe. Grandpa Giovanni smiled and handed me a glass of dark red stuff.

"For you, Kachada," Grandpa said.

"Urako." Realizing I had spoken Comanche, I repeated, "Thank you."

Grandpa laughed. *"Graze.* I will teach you to speak Italian."

The room laughed and made toasts. "Kachada, may you be blessed with good health, happiness, and good fortune." They drank the wine. I mimic them, taking a sip, introducing my taste buds to the tart world of Chianti wine.

From ages ten to nineteen, I lapped up all the Sicilian hugs and kisses my grandparents smothered me with. They taught me to speak several languages working with them on their import and export business. They also spoiled me rotten. They saved me from of a number of tight squeezes, from jumping the local train with my best friend Little to taking a police car for a joyride. That was when Grandpa decided to nicknamed me *JT – just trouble.*

To my Comanche family, I was Kachada: *white man.* To my Sicilian grandparents and my friends in Franklin, I was *JT, "Just Trouble."* Not exactly what my mother expected of me when they took the time to teach me their import business from the ground up, in order to impress upon me the concept of responsibility, respect, and loyalty—not much different from the ideals Chief Peta instilled in me.

When I turned fourteen, my grandparents took me with them to another part of the world, Sicily. I was uncertain of what to expect.

I stared out the window from my seat, never taking my eyes off the blue sky, clouds, and nightlights of the cities below. Another view of how big the world was. When we arrived at the airport in Palermo we were greeted at the gate by my father's cousin Franco.

He was an enormous barrel-chested man. He gave me a bear hug followed by a kiss. "Follow me," Cousin Franco said leading us out the terminal exit to a shiny '57 Chevy convertible. He drove us through the night to the small village of Messina. An older woman gave Giovanni and Isabel a hug and kiss. "This must be Kachada," the woman said.

"Yes ma'am." She kissed and hugged me. "Call me Aunt Concettina, she said. "Come. You all must be hungry."

I soon learned everyone in the family had the prefix *cousin, aunt, or uncle* attached to his or her name.

The next morning I followed the smell fresh of bread and to the Tuscan-style kitchen where Aunt Concettina seemed to live.

After breakfast, it was time to say goodbye to Aunt Concettina, and we crammed into Cousin Franco's convertible. We drove down a narrow road. I was surprised to see people coming to touch cousin Franco's hand. Then we drove on for days stopping along the way to show me the historic sites before we stopped at a place called Nova Gorcia, along the northern border of Italy.

I set out early that morning to watch the sunrise on a hillside. It was a Comanche ritual Chief Peta had taught me, a peaceful way to start every day; he would take me to sit atop Mount Pinchot in the Wichita Mountains overlooking the valley of the Comanche reservation. After the sunrise, I was walking back to the villa when I noticed cousin Franco in the distance talking to two locals in a beat-up Ford hardtop. I sensed this peaceful day was about to turn into trouble.

Suddenly cousin Franco grabbed the driver's head and violently slammed his face into the steering wheel again and again. With each violent blow, blood sprayed onto the windshield. I froze, not knowing what to do. The frightened passenger pulled out a small pistol and shot Franco in his chest. After the shot I jumped, and ran towards him. While bleeding from his chest, Franco took the passenger's hand and snapped his wrist. The sound was so loud I could hear it. Cousin Franco grasped the man's neck, squeezing his throat with his massive hand until the passenger's face turned several shades of red. The man dropped onto the dashboard. I stopped running and watched as my gentle cousin Franco killed a person with his bare hands. It was a bloody scene engraved on my mind.

The sound of gunshots brought the others outside. They struggled to carry three-hundred-pound cousin Franco inside as he pressed his bloody hands against his chest. Family members then returned, driving the hardtop with the two dead passengers away, never to be seen again.

I nervously waited before I continued on. I was shaking from the horrible sight, afraid they would be angry if they knew I saw cousin Franco get shot. When I got inside, I startled everyone. Auntie Biagi said nothing, but immediately kissed me. She took me by my collar and sat me in front of a plate of busiate with pesto trapanese.

I had witnessed the quick and brutal justice of the Sicilian Mafia, a side of the Mafia I had not seen. The side my gentle Grandpa Giovanni never showed me until much later. The word Mafia now had a new meaning to me.

Math and science had always been easy for me. At sixteen, I graduated from high school with honors and earned two scholarships: one in journalism and the other as a member of the NCAA Division of the track and field team at Duquesne University in Pittsburgh, thanks to my photographic memory and my mother's natural athletic ability. I had dreams of becoming a neurosurgeon and at the same time, I worshiped contemporary journalists like Hunter S. Thompson. My world shone brightly and I became blinded with exciting thoughts of what my future could be.

Then life introduced another obstacle. First it was dad dying of a heart attack, and then during my senior year in college, I made an appointment with our family doctor for flu-like symptoms over the Christmas break. Dr. Myers suggested I have an X-ray of my throat as a precaution. It wasn't until after New Year's when Dr. Myers called me to his office. Sitting in the examination room, my mother wore her lab coat as Dr. Myers arrived. I felt uneasy as my mom stepped closer to my side. Dr. Myers turned the lightbox on, revealing numerous X-rays of my neck taken from various angles. He said, *"Kachada you have cancer, my associates and I give you two years to live. I'm sorry to say, but that's being optimistic."*

My mind did something foreign to me. It stopped. I couldn't make it move forward or rewind. Dr. Myers went on to say, "However, there is a new experimental procedure that looks promising. I can't tell you what to do, but you should give this new procedure called radiation a try." I looked at Mom, who remained stoic.

Dr. Myers explained, "The idea of radiation is to kill the cancer before cancer kills you. Kachada, you have what we call lymphoma, part of a group of blood cancers developed in your lymphatic system; your specific type is called Hodgkin's lymphoma." Dr. Myers ended by saying, "Even with this treatment there is only a three percent survival rate."

I remained emotionless. My mind drifted off, *viewing scenes from my most recent past, Chief Peta, Kele, the colorful sunset and sunrises at the reservation. My Sicilian family taking turns hugging and kissing me, feeding me pasta and Chianti.*

Doctor Myers voice brought me back to reality saying, "We might be able to buy you some time. It could be a month or ten years or who knows, but I can't promise how much—if any. The procedure is new and untested. We are one of the first Universities to explore it," he added.

I sat, frozen, unable to respond. All I could think of was my mother's words at birth: *"Remember, birth is a death sentence. So make every minute count."* Those haunting words now became real. From that moment on, I refused to think about the two years and decided 1,051,200 minutes sounded more encouraging. I vowed to battle for every minute beyond the 1,051,200 minutes Doctor Myers sentenced me with. Chief Peta taught me, *"To survive in this beautiful world you have to kill the ugly beasts that live within it."* Well, it looked like I found the answer to that ugly beast. Cancer.

After my radiation treatment, my muscled body started showing the ugly after-effects. From my chest to my chin, my body took on a bone-like appearance. My voice became raspy like a smoky-throated blues singer. I had been taking 5,200 rads of cobalt to my chest, neck, and diaphragm area with each treatment. The 1973 equipment was anything but accurate; giving me second-degree burns over thirty percent of my body. Doctor Myers told me not to concern myself about the scarring. I read between the lines and knew he didn't expect me to live long enough to face them. My dreams were gone and my nightmare began.

I made a promise to myself to live every minute of my life fearlessly and without remorse. I wanted to punish the world. I took a job at Goldstein's Bar as a bouncer to feed my anger. Every day I prepared for work as a warrior going into battle.

One particular night, it was unusually quiet—until the glow of a full moon brought in an outlaw biker wearing the colors of a local gang on his worn jean vest. On his back was emblazed a skull and crossbones with a pirate hat, a symbol of his gang's violent history. The beefy man smelled like last week's garbage. He entered with clenched, club-like fists, slamming through the door, trying to evoke the image of a tough guy. He stalked up to the bar, slammed his helmet down, and shouted in a gravelly voice, "Where's Sarah? Where's Sarah?"

The patrons had no idea who Sarah was. They continued to drink at the bar unfazed.

This made the fat biker even more irate. Frustrated, he stumbled over to the jukebox, mumbling, and ranting to himself. He yanked the plug out of the wall, turning it silent. His attempts to get everyone's attention failed, and when no one looked at him, he picked up an empty bottle from a vacant tabletop and smashed it against the wall.

I'd had enough and I stood up at the other end of the bar. He screamed, "I'm going to kill someone if you don't tell me where Sarah is!"

I couldn't ignore the tempting offer. I walked over and stood face-to-face. "Go ahead," I said.

His red eyes enlarged to the size of quarters and said, "You want me to start with you, asshole?"

I gave him my ice-cold stare and said, "Go ahead kill someone."

He turned to walk away, suddenly he turned, throwing a sloppy Hollywood haymaker. I stepped to my left, leaving him catching nothing but air. He lurched forward and fell on his face, knocking over a chair. He managed to get up and stumbled toward me, taking a switchblade from his jean vest. I caught his meaty arm before he could open it, and bent it in half until I heard it snap. The tough guy gave out a shrilling scream as I bounced him back to the floor.

The fingers on his other hand scrambled for his switchblade. I warned him not to get up.

The fool snarled and opened the knife as he stood up. I threw my forearm into his face and knocked him out. His face and arm were bleeding from the blows. I screamed, "I told you not to get up."

Lester, the bartender, came from behind the bar and took the biker's knife, then propped up his head. He stretched his right ear out like Silly Putty, and sliced it off, admiring it as if it was the Lombardi Trophy.

"Lester, what the fuck are you doing?" I yelled.

Lester replied with his Porky the Pig lisp, "Pickle it." He summoned two patrons to drag the man outside.

That fat biker never returned.

Fights became common, and my reputation as a tough guy spread, prompting others to find out for themselves. I enjoyed the continuous challenge of tossing them out one by one, with one less body part than they came in with. Every person I tossed out of the bar was like a victory, defeating the minutes that were trying to take me.

One night after tossing out another challenger, a patron sitting at the bar handed me a card. It was emblazoned with *LUPO DI SALVO, V.P., Business Relations for the Franklin Collection Agency*. He suggested I give him a call. I'd never heard of such a company and tossed the card into the trash. Weeks later I tossed out yet another challenger and decided to end the madness. I said goodbye to Lester and Goldstein's Bar.

A week later the shrill sound of the phone ringing woke me. I tried to clear my eyes as I reached for it. With my head still buried under the oversized pillows, I put it to my ear and heard a deep voice trying to speak English.

"Kachada," growled a thick Sicilian accent.

I sat up, demanding, "Who is this?"

"Lupo."

Annoyed, I shouted, "I don't fucking know you," and hung up, muttering, *"Asshole."* I fell back to sleep, only to have the phone ring again. Pissing me off. I answered it screaming, "Look fucker . . ."

"JT," the voice said.

"Grandpa?" I asked.

"JT. I have always been there to protect you as a boy. Right?" Grandpa asked.

"Yes. Yes, of course you have, Grandpa," I said.

"Lupo is going to call you again. Lupo is part of the family. If you are determined to live recklessly then I want you where you belong, with the family. I trust Lupo to watch over you. When he calls, answer." All I heard next was the dial tone.

It was less than thirty-seconds before the phone rang. I picked it up. The thick Sicilian accent said, "I will be there in fifteen minutes. Be ready."

I hurried to get dressed and began brushing my teeth before the doorbell rang. Afraid to keep him waiting, I spit into the sink and made a beeline to the door. To my surprise, he wasn't the man who had handed me the card at Goldstein's Bar. He wasn't what I expected. He didn't look anything like his tough-sounding voice on the phone and certainly not dangerous. Lupo was a handsome, slim, dark-haired man with small features and a bright smile holding a dry cleaning hanger. He stood all of five-feet-six-inches; I towered over him. I'm sure my six-foot-plus frame, shoulder-length blond hair, ice-cold blue eyes, and porcelain skin was not what he was expecting.

"Ready?" Lupo asked.

I slipped my black leather jacket over my white t-shirt and started for the door saying, "Yes."

Lupo held up his thin hand. "No. You are not ready. You need a shirt with a collar." He pointed to his starched white button-down shirt, tucked into his black dress pants. I stood there thinking, *I didn't own such a thing*.

He smiled, "Mr. Giovanni said you would need this." He handed me a white starched shirt still on the dry cleaning hanger. I changed, wet my hair and combed it straight back, tucked the long ends behind my ears, then put on my leather jacket over my new starched button-down shirt. I returned for Lupo's review.

He gave me the nod of approval, then told me to always be dressed like a businessman when he came for me. We left, descending the flight of stairs from my apartment. I climbed into his black Buick Riviera and into the scent of new leather. "Sweet. *Very* sweet ride," I said.

Lupo put in a cassette tape and out came the song, *Bad, Bad Leroy Brown*, off we drove. He surprised me, holding out a small mirror with a line of coke. I gladly took a hit. I knew then Lupo and I were going to make a good team. We drove toward Route 62 to Buffalo Street, a quaint part of town where the old timers sat on benches at Fountain Park and watched the unemployed aimlessly stroll by. The bright blue-sky was a rare sight in Franklin. The area was notorious for having no more than forty-five days of sun—leaving the rest of the year overcast, covered with either a mixture of fog and rain or a foot of snow.

Once we took the Buffalo Street exit, I asked where we are going? Lupo said. "We have some furniture business to take care of." He pulled into Fritz Furniture just off 13th and Elk Street and drove to the back of parking lot where the delivery trucks were loading and unloading. Together we walked to the loading dock while workers eyeballed us.

Lupo ignored them, opened the steel door of the warehouse, and walked in. He called out speaking French, "Mr. Carlisle Buteau."

Out came a large Frenchman standing close to seven feet tall. He had giant-like features. His eyes were narrow and dark skin was under his long stringy black hair. He had hands resembling anvils. He had to be wearing custom-made clothes to fit his thick legs and square body.

He stepped up to Lupo, speaking French, "Mr. Buteau is not in right now, but he'll be back around two today."

Lupo politely said, "Thank you. I will return after two."

The large man didn't move. We turned to leave and in a sudden panther-like move, Lupo grabbed an unwrapped bedpost leaning against the wall. He leaped into the air like Bruce Lee and swung the post, striking the right side of the Frenchman's huge head. The man fell to the cement floor making a loud thud; blood spit out of the side of his forehead. Lupo turned to me and said, "Stay here." He dashed into the office across the dock.

The workers paused, looking at the Frenchman lying in the doorway. I took a self-defensive stance, but no one blinked an eye. They turned away and continued working as though nothing had happened. I assumed the Frenchman wasn't very popular.

After a few crashes and a thud, Lupo walked out carrying a *shoebox* in his right hand. He wiped his jet-black hair from his dark eyes with his left hand. It was then I realized he was not only a handsome man but a *fucking dangerous one as well.*

"You did a good job, Kachada," Lupo said.

I admired this fearless man and asked him to call me JT. Lupo frowned, wrinkling his forehead, confused. *"Just Trouble,"* I explained.

He gave me a slap on the back. "JT." We walked back to his Riviera. Once inside, he locked the doors, handed me the shoebox and said, "Count it."

I opened the box and saw fistfuls of five hundred dollar bills, each neatly rolled in a rubber band. "Fuck, a hundred grand!" I shouted.

Lupo said, "Good, Mr. Giovanni will be happy." We made a few more stops that day but none as exciting as the first. It was a routine; Lupo would walk in asking for the owner. The owner or person at the door would come out and hand Lupo a shoebox. Then they shook hands and we left. Clean and fast. By the end of the day, we had collected two hundred and fifty grand. Not bad for four hours of work.

Afterward, Lupo dropped me at my apartment and said, "I will pick you up in a few days." Then handed me a roll of hundred dollar bills and said, "Good job today, JT." And drove off.

After two months of working with Lupo, I had become accustomed to expecting the unexpected.

Team Lupo and JT had become the feared duo for grandpa's business relationship team. We were treated with respect whenever we arrived to collect. I faced every encounter fearlessly. The job came with a few christening scars I was proud to have earned.

The money I earned burned a hole in my pocket so I decided to treat myself to a new candy-apple red Camaro Z28. I paid cash and had the dealer add pipes that started with a purr and grew to a roar and with a Bose sound system I christened it with the cool vibe of Marvin Gaye's "Let's Get It On" as I drove it off the lot.

Cruising through the city with the windows down and the summer breeze blowing through my hair, I snorted the cocaine-laced nasal spray that had become my travel companion and best friend. It helped me to escape the painful effects the radiation had left me with. When I returned to my apartment, I had a message waiting for me from Lupo instructing me to meet him at Fencik's Moving Company the next morning.

We met at 1st and Darr Street, just off the shore of the Allegheny River in Oil City. It was an ugly, dirty, wet drive with the usual gray, overcast day. When I arrived, Lupo climbed out of his Riviera as it started to rain. I told him I had a bad notion about this one.

Lupo looked around the warehouse property and said, "JT, we've got a job to do."

At the service entrance, I pounded on the metal door with my fist, making a noise that echoed through the alley. I waited for a few minutes, watching Lupo get irritated. A short black man opened the door. He stared at us before speaking German. I understood

German, but Lupo didn't. He called out "The collectors are here!"

A voice from the back said in German, "Open the door, then step to the right."

I knew that meant trouble and took the man by his hair, and slammed the door so hard that the sharp metal sliced into his neck. His head became a permanent fixture to the door. Blood spewed everywhere. Lupo ran to the window alongside the building. He pulled out his Glock, and jumped onto the landing, kicking a hole in the window.

I wasted no time. I took the handle of the door, forcing it open with the man's head still attached. I stepped through the puddles of blood dripping from the man's head and rolled to my left. Then I heard the sound of a pin being pulled and a crash. It was a grenade tossed through the window where I last saw Lupo. The explosion spread mortar into the room. Filled with emotion, I jumped to my feet like a madman. I ran to where the grenade was thrown, shooting everything in sight, envisioning Lupo lying dead on the stoop. My line of sight was filled with smoke coming from the barrel of my Beretta.

Two men near the office were lying on the floor, shot. I turned to see two more running towards a stairway door. I pointed my Beretta and then watched them run out the back door. I could have shot them, but I didn't. In one quick motion, I returned to the office, where one of the two was dead, and the other was barely alive. I shoved my Beretta into his mouth. He began to cry, shaking his head back and forth, pleading for his life. *I could only see Lupo, lying dead from the grenade blast.* But I couldn't kill him and I ran outside, fearing I would find Lupo's body on the dock. I found him stunned, but alive. Relief washed over my adrenaline-charged body.

I reached for his arm and screamed, "Lupo, let's go." He got up and pulled away, insisting he needed to go inside. I hesitated but followed him. The other workers had run off. Lupo entered the office and I heard two rounds fired. He emerged with a shoebox under his armpit and his Glock. I asked, "What happened?"

Lupo said, "One was alive." I knew then I should have shot him. I didn't mention the two that ran out the back door.

We were prepared to fight our way out. I followed him, backing up past the head stuck to the door as workers came out of hiding. We left the warehouse without any other incidents.

Once outside, Lupo handed me the shoebox, asking me to deliver it to my grandpa. When he opened his car door I noticed his left hand was hanging by only muscle. Blood was pouring from his wrist. I tried yelling out to him, but he sped off, leaving me shouting for him to stop. Worried about the others in the warehouse, I got into my car and started driving towards Franklin. From out of nowhere, flashing red lights came up behind me. I pulled into a drive-thru, thinking they were going to stop me. But it was my lucky day as the police car drove on. I let out a sigh of relief as the drive-thru menu sign welcomed me to Arby's. I drove through and parked in the Arby's lot. I was feeling the after-effects of seeing the man's head attached to the door. I opened my car door and threw up. I gathered myself and jotted down two hundred grand in the collection book. Once I got to Grandpa's, I handed him the shoebox along with the collection book and asked if he knew anything about Lupo.

Grandpa saw how distraught I was and said, "Lupo has to have his hand amputated. My doctors are working on him as we speak."

Hearing this news, my heart dropped. I knew it was just a matter of time considering the business we were in. Now I had seen both sides of the Mafia family. Grandpa assured me that Lupo and his family would be taken care of.

Grandpa said, "JT, this is not for you." He handed me three rolls of five hundred dollar bills from his wall safe behind the painting of Mother Mary and said, "Time has come for you to leave Franklin and stop running from life and start chasing the life you have left."

He was right. I thought I was a badass until I had to kill another human being. I gave him a kiss and a hug and walked out the door. Grandpa followed, watching me from the porch steps. I forced a smile knowing he had always been there to protect me. Now it was time I survive on my own. I cranked up "Live And Let Die" by Guns n' Roses, to clear my head and drove off. I left my career in Business Relations behind, but not the memories of my friend Lupo or the bloody head attached to the door.

"Mr. Toscano, Sorry to interrupt but I'm sure you won't mind," Senator Cornwall said. "I am told your scotch has arrived." The senator signals Jon.

Jon scurries in and sets the bottle of Macallan 'M' and a faceted glass down and leaves. Pouring the rich amber color into the glass, I could hear Jean-Pierre, *I warn you, Kachada, after your first sip any other will be disappointing*. I raised my glass, "Thank you, Senators."

CHAPTER 6

November 30, 1973,
Lawton, Oklahoma

I spend two days on the road before I pulled up to my grandpa's small wood home. It had been ten years since I had returned to the reservation. There he was sitting on the porch. The strong man with thick hands and eyes of steel was not as I remembered him. I stared at the gray-haired man from my car as the Chief stood up to welcome me home. When he placed his once very heavy hands on my shoulder it hit me walking inside. The great Comanche warrior Chief Peta had become an old man.

It had been two years since his fifth wife Asdza's spirit joined her ancestors. Asdza was a young Osage Indian girl he captured during a Comanche raid. He saved her from being tortured by the others and took her as one of his wives.

Historians labeled the Osage Indians as one of the most handsome tribes of the Indian Nations. The men stood up to seven feet tall. Asdza was five feet eleven inches tall. She left behind a granddaughter, Aponi, raised after her daughter Ela died during childbirth.

I entered grandpa's home and saw a tall young girl. She wasn't like anyone I had ever seen before. Her flawless skin glowed against her thick black hair and black almond-shaped eyes. She was so beautiful I found it hard to breathe.

Grandpa introduced her. "Kachada, this is Aponi." She stood close to six feet tall. Then he introduced me, "Aponi, this is Kachada."

"Chief Peta spoke often of you." The soft smoky texture of her voice made me quiver. I nodded and moved on to Grandpa, trying to break her spell. But my eyes danced over every inch of her tall beautiful frame as she left Grandpa and me alone.

After a dinner of cornbread and honey-glazed chicken baked over an open fire, I bedded down feeling guilty for thinking of my grandma's homemade Sicilian bread, pasta, wine, and the beautiful Aponi.

The next morning the aroma of cooking drew me to the kitchen. There, Aponi was wrapping fresh hot corn tortillas. She wore tight blue jeans and sneakers. Her long hair was braided in an Indian-style ponytail wrapped in a beaded headband. Grandpa's painting of Chief Quanah was silkscreened onto the back of her dark blue jersey.

I flashed a smile when she surprised me with a warm taco and said, "For your trip to the mountain."

I was surprised she knew of my morning ritual and thanked her, but my eyes were saying something else as I took the taco and left for the mountains to watch the sunrise.

Sitting high above the reservation on Mount Pinchot, I watched the enchanted sunrise and reflected on the strange intersection of my Comanche and Sicilian ancestry. I had developed a fierce devotion to my past, my family, the Mafia and Comanche ideals of honor and justice. I closed my eyes smelling the earth taking me back to when I was seven years old sitting in Grandpa's studio. *I sat on my stool next to him. He handed me an old scrap of plywood, one of his old hawk feathers, chunk of torn plasterboard painted white with a hole cut in it for my thumb and said, "Kachada, paint." I froze looking at the blank section of wood. "Don't be afraid. Make this piece of wood whatever you want it to be. Attack it."*

I began to play with colors, moving them from one place to another, adding blue, then green and red, as I moved the colors from one end of the board to the next. I had no idea what I was doing but I whatever it was excited me. I was so engaged I forgot Grandpa was there.

I kept staring at the painted plywood. "I felt excited and I didn't know why."

Grandpa put his hand on my shoulder and said, "You will learn art is a powerful medicine."

A medicine I became addicted to.

I returned to the village to say good-bye to Grandpa and the beautiful Aponi before I headed one hundred ninety miles south to Dallas. I was ready to leave my angry life behind, knowing I had 613,200 minutes left from my sentence of 1,052,200. I turned up the volume of "Ramblin' Man" by The Allman Brothers Band to drown out the thought of my constant companion, time.

CHAPTER 7

December 3, 1973, Dallas, Texas

My first stop in Dallas was Sonny Bryant's BBQ. It had been written up as President Lyndon Johnson's favorite lunch stop when in Dallas. It was an unusually warm sunny day when I pulled into the dirt parking lot and found an odd combination of suits and ties, big hair, cowboy hats, and families sitting on the bumpers of pickup trucks parked respectfully side-by-side, devouring the ribs.

Inside were handwritten menus behind the long narrow ordering window. BBQ this and that delivered the aroma of sweet herbs, spices, freshly baked bread and mesquite wood hovering over the hungry customers.

The line moved quickly but never dwindled as each customer left another arrived taking their place in line.

"Your order?" asked the order-taker.

"Ah, yes. Not sure what to order," I said.

He called out, "Number eight basket. You want a longneck?"

"A longneck?" I asked.

The man shouts, "One cold longneck. That's six bucks."

I handed him a ten and said, "Keep the change, cowboy."

He never smiled or acknowledged the tip and he handed me my longneck with a basket of ribs, corn on the cob, fried okra and several packets of wipes.

I sat on my candy apple red Z28 bumper and began to ravage the beef ribs falling off the bone. I couldn't get enough of the sweet BBQ taste and licked it off my fingers. After I took the last the ice-cold sip of my longneck I drove to the Mansion Hotel. Texas was quickly becoming my kind of place - cowboys, BBQ, and ice-cold beer.

The Mansion was everything Sonny Bryant's was not, a luxurious hotel where the beautiful people stayed when visiting big "D." I decided to claim it as my home. When not rubbing elbows with the beautiful clientele, I partied around town, discovering the underbelly of Dallas's steamy nightlife. Then late one afternoon, after a long night of clubbing, I sat alone at the hotel bar relaxing with my Bloody Mary to clear my head. In walked a well-dressed man with the audacity to plop himself right next to me. Judging by the slim, well-tailored suit and his mannerisms, it was obvious to me he was European. "Hello," the man said smiling.

After I heard his thick French accent, I used it as an excuse to show off my French, "Salut, comment allez-vous?" He was delighted to speak his home tongue. We enjoyed talking about the many wonderful attractions Dallas had to offer. We got lost in our conversation, running into the early evening when he asked me, "Aimeriez-vous vous joinder à moi pour le dîner?" *To join him for dinner.*

Caught by surprise, I asked, "Où puis-je demander?" *Where, may I ask?'* He looked at his watch and said he had reservations at the French Room. The five-star restaurant was famous for its six-course dinner and overly expensive wine list. I found him to be interesting enough, so figured why not and said, "Qui."

"Would you please call a driver for us?" The smiling man asked the bartender. Then introduced himself, "I am Jean-Pierre."

I shook his hand and I said, "Kachada Toscano."

He was fascinated by my name. We made small talk during the ride to the French Room. When we arrived, the traditional white-jacketed waiter with a black bow tie escorted us to a white-clothed table. He perched about three feet back as our Sommelier, wearing a wine opener around his neck, ready to tend to our every need. It was quite a picture. Each table had a Sommelier in a white jacket standing at attention. Jean-Pierre and I spent hours chatting over glasses of fine wine and every sumptuous bite of our six-course dinner. We absorbed ourselves in conversation about my favorite subjects: art and fast cars.

Jean-Pierre Caron said, "Kachada, I am ejoying your company."

"Yes, I am as well Jean-Pierre. Why are you in Dallas?" I asked.

"To cover a story for my magazine. I am writing an article on Mario Ferrari."

"A writer?" I asked.

"Yes, but it was not what I started out to be. Kachada, what is it you do?" Jean-Pierre asked.

I didn't know what to say, so I said "An adventurist." It was somewhat true. I just left out the reason why.

"An adventurist. Have you read RACE?" Jean-Pierre asked.

"I have. I have indeed," I said.

Then Jean-Pierre said, "I started out as a Grand Prix Driver, but after my first year I had an unfortunate collision and it cost me my career."

"Jean-Pierre, sorry to hear that," I said.

He nodded and said, "The doctors told me I could keep driving, but if I had another collision it could cost me my life. So I did what anyone who loves life would do. I followed my mistress, and created a racing magazine."

"Jean-Pierre, RACE is not just a racing magazine. It's the bible for the Grand Prix."

"That is kind of you," Jean-Pierre said. He smiled said and asked, "I would like to know about Kachada?"

We had more in common than fast cars and art. But I didn't feel the need to tell him. "Like you, I started out working towards my dreams of becoming a neurosurgeon, but then I got sidetracked."

"Sidetracked? What is sidetracked?" Jean-Pierre asked.

"Going a different direction than you intended," I replied.

" Ah, what?"

"My first love is art. My grandpa introduced me to art. Since then it has become a passion of mine," I said.

"Kachada, I too love art and, of course fast cars." Then he told me about his family. "My father wanted me to take over the family business. We have a very successful winery in the south of France. Caron Vineyards. My name is Jean-Pierre Caron. Perhaps you have heard of it?" he asked.

"Sorry, but no," I apologized.

Jean-Pierre shrugged his shoulders and said, "My father was not happy when I chose to become a Grand Prix driver. But I was young and rebellious. I love wine. But I don't care to make it. Did you say your grandfather is a painter?" he asked.

I played the namedropper game and said, "Comanche Chief Peta. He is known throughout Europe. Perhaps you have heard of him?"

His eyes light up, as I knew they would. "Yes, I do know of him, you are his grandson? Are you Comanche? What does Kachada mean?" Jean-Pierre was so excited he couldn't stop asking me questions.

"Yes to all of the above. Kachada means white man," I said.

"I don't understand. You don't look like any American Indian I have seen on TV," Jean-Pierre said with a big grin.

I too grinned and said, "No. I don't. My mother was Comanche and my father Sicilian."

"Kachada Toscano. Comanche and Sicilian. That is interesting. I am glad we met. Perhaps it was fate," Jean-Pierre said. Then he called the Sommelier over and off he went, returning with a beautifully shaped bottle of scotch.

"Kachada, have you ever tasted Macallan 'M' Scotch?" Jeane-Pierre asked.

"No," I said.

He held up a glass and said, "You must always drink it in a faceted glass." He handed the rich amber colored drink to me. I was about to take a sip when he stopped me and said, "Kachada, I warn you. After your sip, any other will be disappointing."

I nodded and I took a gentle sip. I had never tasted such a smooth rich flavor. From that moment on I became spoiled.

Time had passed when Jean-Pierre apologized and said he had to leave. He had an early morning interview with the family member of Mario Ferrari, who had recently passed away. We finished our last glass of Macallan, compliments of Jean-Pierre, and returned to the hotel.

Waking up late after a night of fine wine and scotch, I spotted an envelope lying under my door.

> I enjoyed your company Mr. Toscano, and I would like to offer you a ticket to join me at the Dallas Museum of Art. The collection of the famed French collector Catherine Bernard is on exhibit, featuring several works by Pablo Picasso.
>
> —Jean-Pierre Caron

I immediately called the front desk and left a message thanking him for the ticket and accepted his invite. Then I ordered a tailor to my room to be fitted for a classic black tuxedo. I had the perfect accent to wear with my tux, my favorite Comanche bolo made of silver and turquoise my grandfather had made.

Arriving at the museum, I introduced myself to the painting *Les Demoiselles D'Avignon,*

considered one of Picasso's most innovative works when Jean-Pierre surprised me. Coming up behind me, Jean-Pierre asked, "Ah, you like naked women?"

I kept my attention on the Picasso and replied, "I prefer mine less distorted." We both had a good laugh.

"Your bolo. The work of Chief Peta?" Jean-Pierre asked.

"Yes it is," I said.

"Exquisite. Kachada, would you like to join me at the bar upstairs?" Jean-Pierre asked.

I followed him to the elevator taking us to the second floor, where art lovers were drinking cocktails and eating finger sandwiches. We sat next to the clear glass railing overlooking the eclectic crowd.

"Kachada, tell me how you came to be in Dallas. I know you say you are an adventurist," Jean-Pierre asked.

Always cautious about telling my tale, I took him through my unusual background of growing up as a Comanche warrior and being raised by my Sicilian grandfather, omitting my cancer diagnosis. He was infatuated, and then he caught me off guard.

"We both love art and, most importantly, fast cars. I find you a very interesting and well-spoken man," Jean-Pierre said.

Jean-Pierre was an easy person to like. "Thank you," I replied.

"Kachada, I have been searching for a writer to cover the upcoming Grand Prix Racing Circuit. I know we just met, but I think you could be that person," Jean-Pierre said.

I was flustered and didn't know what to say. "Jean-Pierre, I've never worked as a writer before."

Jean-Pierre smiled and said, "Kachada, I have been looking for a fresh new perspective to cover the 1974 Formula One Circuit, someone who would deliver a unique flavor to the international event. I think that someone could be you Kachada. You appear to be a natural fit, you speak several languages and you love the sport."

I couldn't believe what I was hearing. I was excited and depressed at the same time.

"Does this interest you? Or am I wrong?" Asked Jean-Pierre.

I had to contain my excitement and said, "I'm sure there are well-seasoned writers out there who would love the opportunity to work for you and your magazine."

"There are, but they bore me," Jean-Pierre said. "I don't need another boring writer. Kachada, you may not have experience writing about the Grand Prix, but you are most certainly not boring. You Kachada, are different. I like different. Would you consider it?" Jean-Pierre asked.

My mind did a rapid rewind of my life up to this point. Journalism was my second major and now I was being offered a dream I shouldn't resist. I needed to go for it. I took a deep breath and said, "Yes, I am interested."

Jean-Pierre was excited as he raised his glass of Champagne. "Kachada, you have no idea how happy you just made me." Then he launched right into business. "The first race is in Buenos Aires on January 13. I would need to have an article about the drivers and the race on the magazine stands before the race, for the February issue. Leaving you only a few weeks left to party."

I realized the magnitude of the offer. Knowing my battle with time, I began to second-guess my reply. Jean-Pierre must have seen my hesitation. He reached into his tuxedo jacket and pulled out a check sliding it across the table, saying, "Consider this a signing bonus. It pays twenty-grand a week for the twenty-six week season all expenses are included."

Jean-Pierre had handed me a check made out for one hundred thousand dollars. Obviously, he had given the decision great thought. Then he said, "I am leaving tomorrow evening for Paris. Kachada I am so excited about the two of us working as a team." Before excusing himself to attend to other guests, he reminded me, "You are what my magazine has been looking for."

According to Doctor Myers, I didn't have enough time left to cover the yearlong Grand Prix. But, like grandpa Giovanni said, *"it was time to start chasing the life I had left."*

CHAPTER 8

December 28, 1973,
Dallas, Texas

After accepting Jean-Pierre's offer I remained at the Mansion until he sent me an airline ticket along with accommodations at the New Sheraton Buenos Aires Hotel in Argentina for the inaugural race of the 1974 Formula One Racing season. This was my first south of the equator. The nineteenth-century buildings, the iconic balconied presidential palace in Buenos Aires was a bustling city full of life, making for a colorful introduction to South America.

It was ten days after New Year's and the Formula One Grand Prix Racing Circuit party had started. Crowds filled the hotels along with expensive wine, vodka, and Dom Perignon, staples of the racing circuit. The party continued to São Paulo, where I enjoyed my first taste of the local favorite Caipirinha. It is considered Brazil's most popular drink, made with Cachaça, similar to white rum, with sugar and lime.

The race was given little attention outside the racing groupies. The only drama unfolding was Emerson Fittipaldi the popular Brazilian driver within the home crowd but not beyond their own borders. His win in Sao Paulo gave the partygoers in Brazil a reason to continue their party to the next race in the Kyalami Circuit in Johannesburg, South Africa. Known as one of the favorites for the Grand Prix beach lovers.

A week before the race from my balcony at the Table Bay Hotel, I took in the exotic landscape of horizontal tanning beauties covering the sandy beaches of the Cape. The lobby was filling up with faces I recognized from Sao Paolo. The Fittipaldi's followers brought their party a week before the race. The endless flow of beautiful women kept arriving looking for their next adventure.

Before the sunrise, I was on the beach doing my martial arts routine of basic stretches to keep my leg from becoming stiff. Then I heard, "Hallo."

I opened my eyes. To my delight, there stood a dark-haired beauty in a tiny bikini smiling. Her accent was German. "Du bist wunderschön." *You are very beautiful.* I said.

She told me her name was Urska and I replied, "Wenig zu entblößen." *Little to bare.* She put on a strong flirtatious pose and introduced her fellow joggers. "Das ist Agata und da ist Zala." *This is Agata and Zala.*

I flirted back, "Gut und schön." *Good and Beautiful.* The women giggled like schoolgirls. We became instant friends and walked along the beach as the sun rose, cuddling and swimming in the ocean, making my first adventure to the Cape a memorable one.

Urska asked me if I would escort Agata and Zala to the Esmeralda party. I asked, "What is Esmeralda?"

Urska replied, "A yacht owned by a Russian billionaire."

"Why, is it dangerous for you to go alone?" I asked.

Urska said, "Bravta. Not nice people. With you, we will feel safer."

"How do you know he's mafia?"

She laughed, "He is a billionaire. Russian billionaires are Bratva.

"Should be fun. Yes," I said.

"I promise, you will enjoy it." We kissed and turned back to frolicking on the beach.

Peering through the bright sun a waiter in a white coat and black tie, carrying a silver platter engraved with the emblazoned logo of the Esmeralda, stopped to offer a bottle of Armand de Brignac surrounded by fluted Swarovski champagne glasses. We enjoyed the bubbly as I laid on the sun deck of the Esmeralda with three beautiful Slovenian girls.

After one too many bubblies, I need to get up and move my leg and take a walk as the girls in their lounge chairs were still sleeping.

Finishing off an entire bottle of Champagne will do that to you. I took a walk to the other side of the deck. Standing along the railing, I heard a desperate voice crying out in Slovak, "You will pay for this! Don't," followed by two quick pops and a splash. I recognized the sound - a small caliber semi-automatic pistol. I moved toward the noise taking me to the captain's deck. Two dark-skinned men were looking over the side. One spotted me and shouted in German, "What are you doing here?"

I recognized the Belgium dialect and pretended I *didn't* understand.

They approached, repeating: "What are you doing here?" I shook my head, acting confused. They stood in front of me discussing if they should kill me or not. So I kept playing dumb, they decided I was and moved on.

I smiled, speaking English as I gave them the typical American cliché, "Have a nice day."

They turned looking at me and muttered, "Arschloch." *Asshole.*

I immediately descended to the deck below. I looked over the side, knowing someone was pleading for his life. But there was no sign of blood or a body. I returned to the girls and found the same Belgians talking to them. I waited in the distance, watching the bare-breasted women convince them they heard nothing. The two men left as Urska, Zala, and Agata resumed sharing a mimosa.

I relaxed in the chaise lounge taking in the warm sun, wondering *who it was they tossed overboard*?

When we dropped anchor, two South African Police officers were questioning the captain. While we de-boarded the yacht, Urska gave me a kiss thanking me for being their escort. I said goodbye to Zala and Agata and returned to my hotel room.

Two days later the Cape Times published an article about a missing ambassador from Czechoslovakia. The local news station reported the missing ambassador was investigating suspicious money laundering to various radical organizations for the United Nations, and he had not been seen since Friday night. I knew the official language of the Czech Republic is Slovak. It's clear to me he could be the one who cried out for help on the Esmeralda.

Carlos Reutemann made headlines when he won the third Grand Prix race. But there were no new headlines about the missing ambassador. After the Esmeralda incident, I deduced the Formula One Racing Circuit not only attracted the international race crowd, but also a potentially dangerous political crowd.

During week twenty-two, after Buenos Aires, Brazil, Spain, South Africa, and Belgium, I was at the granddaddy of them all: Monaco Grand Prix, where the parties were considered the crème de la crème of the Formula One Circuit.

I arrived at the infamous Monte Carlo Casino in a Bentley with a driver. I was wearing my black tux greeted by valets in white coats, who were also escorting drivers and their dates from the likes of a Ferrari 512BB, Lamborghini Countach LP500 S, DeLorean

DMC 12, and Aston Martin V8 Vantage Zagato, to the grand entrance.

The casino resembled a castle, elevated over a long cobblestone drive lined with elegant palm trees. Rows and rows of red roses adorn the lush, landscaped grounds. It gave me goosebumps as I mingled among the sexy elegance, style, money, and royalty. I gazed up at the grand chandeliers with gold leaf accents, crown molding, tall marble columns, and walls anointed with 17th-century works of art perfectly complementing the background of international chatter.

My first stop was the roulette wheel. It was rumored the ball fell on black twenty-six times in a row in 1913. The uncommon occurrence left the professionals gambling in black with a legendary legacy, creating mysticism around the wheel, where gamblers around the world and myself went to pay homage. I was enthralled, watching the payouts to the perfect fitting little black dresses and tuxedos sipping expensive liquor smoking thin, tan, European cigarettes. They created a sophisticated fan base around the green felt table with swirls of smoke drifting up past their lipstick and mustached faces, reminding me of an Edward Hopper painting.

After inhaling the casino smoke for hours, I made my way to the valet to summon my driver. On my way, I noticed reflections of the two Belgians in the glass doors. They were fixed on me entering the Bentley watching my driver speed off, leaving me to wonder *why I had their attention.*

The driver handed me my Strawberry Cough, the cannabis took my mind off the Belgians and the pain in my leg. I had found a published article on early results of massive doses of radiation. They documented patients who were suffering from the effects of nerve damage. The research verified what I already knew my leg was going numb as a direct result of the nerve damage to my spine. It also said the nerve could become brittle over time, making it harder for me to walk and breathe. I was not only battling to outlive my diagnosis, but the possibility of losing mobility in my leg. Smoking weed like Strawberry Cough helped me to control the unpredictable pain reminding me I had used up 744,600 of the 1,051,200 minutes I had left. I inhaled, thinking: *Screw Dr. Myers and his diagnosis. I'll outlive them all.*

At the twelfth race on the circuit driving by the scenery of windmills and tulips replicated the images I recalled from my high school World Geography textbook on my way to Zandvoort in Holland, near Amsterdam. The Hollanders were not as pretentious as the other host cities. The posh parties took a back-seat to the race.

The Sands Hotel in Zandvoort was an upmarket lodge-style hotel with a 400-year old past. In 1948, the Dutch Grand Prix was instrumental in bringing Zandvoort back to life, turning it into an exclusive resort and making the white sandy beaches along the IJmeer Bay one of the most popular beaches in the North Sea.

The next morning I was perched fifty yards back from the water on the Kennemerduinen an der Nordsee beach, exercising my

Comanche ritual, taking in the sunrise and listening to the waves, when a voice cried out. I jumped to my feet to peer through the thick fog in the direction of the cries. Déjà vu. The two Belgians were at it again, attacking a man on the beach. *Who the fuck, were these guys?*

Both were too busy beating the man to notice me approaching. I barked in German, "Halt." They stopped.

As I stepped through the fog into their line of sight, they screamed, "You again."

The man on the ground was bleeding. One of the Belgians pounced on me. I pushed him aside and struck his knee with all of my force. He fell to the ground and pulled a pistol from his pocket. I kicked his hand, knocking it away, and forced my knee into his chest. He grasped my throat. I used a Krav Maga move, twisting his wrist as we both fought for his Mauser lying in the sand next to us. Two shots accidentally fired into his side. I jumped up, looking down at the wounded man, in shock. I heard the other Belgian running off and chased his image, aiming the Mauser, but the fog was too thick, watching him disappear. I returned stumbling over the man they were beating in the fog and checked his pulse. Whoever he was, they had succeeded in killing him.

I kneeled over the Belgian I shot and said, "Warum tust du das?" *Why are you doing this?* His eyes were swollen and glazed. He screamed, "Shafik al-Azor." He muttered "Er wird dich töten." *He will kill you.* Then spit in my face before passing away.

Shafik al-Azor. Wiping the spit from my face I recalled hearing his name in the news while traveling throughout Europe. He was connected to radical terrorist bombings and known for attacks in the Middle East and southern Europe and for revenging the killing of his disciples. I knew if Shafik found out I killed one of his disciples he would be looking for me. I didn't have time to waste and I didn't want to spend it explaining to the local police and taking the chance of exposing my name. I took my rosary, said a prayer for the mystery man they killed and for the dead Belgian. My morning ritual had become a nightmare that would suck me into the dark crevices of the world.

CHAPTER 9

August 30, 1974,
Milan, Italy

Two weeks had gone by, and still, there were no news reports about the dead Belgian and the mystery man. Still nervous about killing a disciple of Shafik, I checked into the luxurious Hotel de la Ville Monza in Milan for the Italian Grand Prix, the thirteenth race. A petite, gray-haired lady at the front desk handed me a sealed envelope labeled in Italian. I unsealed it, revealing a note written by my Grandma Isabel:

Dear JT,

I wish you safe travels. Grandpa Giovanni is not well and wishes to travel to Italy to be buried with his family in Marsala. Grandpa asks if you could come to Marsala to visit him one last time.

Love you,
Grandma Isabel

I struggled to find a chair, and collapsed into it. I called for the valet and requested my bags be taken up to my room. Shutting my eyes, I tried to capture the *smell of the home-made Sicilian pasta, the wine, the overflow of hugs and kisses.* Then I took the next flight to Sicily.

Cousin Franco was waiting at the gate when I arrived at the small airport in Palermo. "Cousin Franco! The last time I was here you had been shot!" I said.

Cousin Franco said, "Your Giovanni told me you were worried. But I am Sicilian, strong!" The only difference between this cousin Franco and the cousin Franco I had met years before was his thick black hair was now thinner and his temples were turning gray.

On the drive to Marsala, cousin Franco explained the seriousness of Grandpa's condition. We pulled up in his shiny black Buick and were greeted by the entire family waiting to smother me with their hugs and kisses. They ushered us into the house where freshly baked bread sat on the long table surrounded by antipasto, arancini—rice balls stuffed with Bolognese sauce and béchamel—calamari, baby artichokes baked with Parmesan, and linguini with red clam sauce and Chianti.

I quietly observed every inch of Grandpa as he walked into the room. Every step was carefully placed. Each of us gave him a gentle hug. He sat in his usual spot, at the head of the table. We began to eat, laughing and reminiscing about Grandpa's beautiful life. I watched him throughout the conversation, absorbing every second, listening to his stories about his sons. He reminded us how much he missed his four sons he had to bury at a young age.

Grandpa gave me a toast, and asked me to join him. I held his wonderful age-spotted hand, never taking my eyes off of him. From the smell of homemade cooking to the smell of ripe grapes and fresh basil from the porch, a view that belonged on a van Gogh canvas.

He held up his glass of wine. "JT, Che dio sia con te." *God be with you.* My eyes began to swell. He put his hand on my face and said, "You are like my very own son, the last son of my family. I have no family other than you and what is here in Marsala. This is where I spent my young life, and I am proud Isabel and I will be buried here alongside my mother, father, and my four sons."

He squeezed my hand. "I do not want you to come to my funeral. I want you to remember this face as we sit here, breathing in the Sicilian air, at home with our family enjoying the Chianti."

Tears streamed down my face as I thought how much this old man meant to me. Each wrinkle on his face told the story of his love for the family and the battles he fought to protect them. He reached into his shirt pocket and handed me an envelope. I started to open it, but he stopped me. "No. After you leave." I kissed him, sobbing like a baby. Our tears mingled. We drank more Chianti and listened to more of his precious stories.

I struggled to wake up when I heard. "Kachada, I must get you to the airport."

The effects from the last night's wine caused me to unknowingly blurt out, "I'm not leaving yet! I came here to visit Grandpa. Cousin Franco, stop shaking me."

"I booked a flight for you," Cousin Franco said. He sat on the edge of my bed. "JT, it's time for you to go."

I reflected on what Grandpa said last night. I knew what I needed to do.

Flying over the green hills and vineyards, I was eating a cheese cannoli Cousin Franco gave me for the trip, thinking of Grandpa, when the pilot announced we should prepare for landing.

Senator Rubin said, "Mr. Toscano. It is very hard to lose a loved one. I must tell you, I find myself sympathizing with your plight."

"Yes," said Senator Cornwall.

"Senators, that will change," I said. They appeared mystified by my answer.

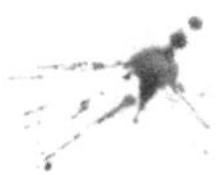

I pulled the folded envelope from my bag in the hotel room and stared at it, not sure I wanted to see what was inside. I put it down and poured a scotch before I finally had the courage to open it. Taking out my Swiss knife, I carefully opened the top, and pulled out a folded yellow notepaper.

Dear JT,

You have made our family proud. I know the pain you must suffer facing every day as if it's going to be your last. My love will be in your heart forever. God has been good to my life. He has provided me with love, family and wealth. Accept this check for two million dollars as a sign of my love. God bless you JT.

—Grandpa

I reread the note over to imagine his voice narrating it. My tears blurred my vision each time I read it. My nose dripped from the sadness I felt. I was losing one of the most important people in my life.

Without hesitation, I took a Swiss Air flight the next morning, and in fifty-five minutes I landed in Zurich. The trains and cyclists were moving along the canal, making for a postcard setting. At Bahnhofstrasse 45, the tall stone column entrance to the UBS resembled something from the Roman Empire. I walked through the arched glass doors into a wide-open marble entrance. My footsteps drowned out the mumbling tellers. I opened the account and deposited the money.

My grandpa took care of everyone around him. My Grandma Isabel would stay in Marsala to live out the rest of her life among the luscious green vineyards of Sicily, waiting to rejoin her Giovanni. My mother flew back to Franklin to sell off Grandpa's businesses, closing all his accounts, and taking over his estate.

On a short walk from the bank, I sat on one of the many wooden benches along the waterfront of the Limmat River's calm current, taking in the aura of the city, thinking of Grandpa. Within minutes a shabbily dressed businessman walked by and sat next to me, a man that would change my life. I didn't like my personal space being invaded by this stranger. Annoyed, I turned and spoke German: "Gibt es einen Grund, warum du hier sitzen?" *Is there a reason why you are sitting here?*

"Yes," the strange man said in English.

His skin was two shades lighter brown than his tattered dark brown jacket. His eyes were slivers making it hard to see their color. He looked to be forty or so years old. His clothes were more business than casual—worn, earth brown wool pants and scuffed black wingtip shoes. His clothes hung on him, one size too big. But his shirt, oddly enough, was starched, presenting a narrow brown tie. His hands were long and lean as was the rest of his body. He smelled of European cigarettes, which were sweeter than our harsh American brands. His teeth were short and yellow, stained from the cigarettes, coffee, and tea making up the European diet. It was an uncontrollable habit of mine to take notes and collect details. But I sensed something special about this person. He might be someone I needed to remember. "What is it you want?" I asked.

He smiled exposing more of his short, yellowed teeth framed with large gums and said, "I am Hayri." Turkish for *man of use*. "I have been watching you since Zandvoort."

I gave him a cold stare thinking, *Who is this person? There was a unique aura about him.*

He quietly said, "I appreciate what you tried to do for Thomas at the beach dunes."

I tried not to look uneasy. I turned to look around, sensing the anxiety of being followed. Hayri gave me a closed smile, appearing to be self-conscious about his yellow teeth. I felt like my identity had been raped. I answered in a slow, deliberate tone, "I don't know what you're talking about, and who is Thomas?"

Hayri said, "The man you tried to save. We share the same enemies."

I was disturbed and frightened by his comment and said, "I have no enemies."

Hayri leaned too close to me and said, "After Zandvoort you do." His eyes opened wider revealing they were brown. Others must be watching us. I scanned the area with only my eyes, careful not to move my head.

He took a business card from his worn brown jacket and handed it to me:

Hayri Sadik
Edelstein Wählen
Natürliche Edlsteine nur
+90 312 213 2965
SETT Co. Ltd 183/24-25 Moo 4,
Trirat Rd, T. Chantanimit A. Muang
Chanthaburi 2200, Thailand

I noticed his name was Sadik, meaning *loyal* in Turkish. "Think about what I said. You can reach me by calling that number on my card."

I returned with, "Why would I need to call you?"

He didn't hesitate. "Because I know all about you. And we both want to find Shafik before he finds you. Shafik is connected to the bastards that took my family from me." He stood up and said, "Again, thank you for trying to save my friend Thomas." Then he turned and walked briskly down the canal with his hands in his jacket pocket and his chin digging into his chest, leaving me with the mystery.

I felt an unnerving chill and tucked the card into my leather jacket.

Lying on the down-feathered king size bed in my hotel, I took a long drag from my hashish pipe, staring at the dark stained ceiling, wondering if this strange Haryi could be a disciple of Shafik pretending to befriend me. I tried not to think about the strange Hayri Sadik and his friend Thomas and nodded off, only to be awakened by the ringing phone. Clumsily I knocked the phone off the hook.

When I recovered, I heard a voice speaking Italian, "JT. It's cousin Franco." I sat up and tried to shake off the effects of the hashish. "JT, I need you to go to Franklin. Your mother needs you at Grandpa's house. You need to leave soon," Cousin Franco said.

Without hesitation, I caught the next twelve-hour Delta flight nonstop to Pittsburgh.

Drained from all the travel and the mysterious call, I worried about Mom. The Hayri character still lurked in the back of my mind as I arrived at the Pittsburgh Airport. I rented a car and drove like a Grand Prix Racer, ignoring every speed limit on the way to Franklin.

An hour later, I bounded up the front porch steps and started to unlock the front door when I heard a voice asking, "Who is it?"

Stunned, I said, "Mom, its Kachada." Mom was a workaholic, leaving me to wonder why she wasn't at work. She opened the door, looking disheveled, as if she hasn't slept for days.

I was relieved to see her and gave her a hug. Then she hugged me back, crying. "Kachada." It was the first time my mother ever hugged me.

"Mom, cousin Franco called and told me to go home. That you needed me." Mom walked me inside and sat down, patting the seat next to her for me to join her. The Comanche way, not over-emotionalizing any feelings. I sat next to her. "Kachada, I am sorry you had to make the trip. But I'm fine," she said.

I knew better than to believe her. "Mom, you are home and you would normally be at work. So something is wrong. You need to tell me," I begged.

Mom was a master at changing the subject. "Kachada are you hungry?" She started to get up.

I stopped her. "Mom, what is it?" I insisted.

Finally, she sat back down and confessed. "I came home two days ago and found a young man going through Grandma's jewelry cases. I screamed at him to leave. He just laughed, put the jewelry in his pocket, and spit in my face."

"Who was it?" I calmly asked.

"I don't know his name, but he is the son of one of Grandpa's employees," Mom said.

By now I was visibly upset. "Can you describe him?" I asked.

"A thin young man with wild red hair," she said rubbing her forehead.

"Mom you need to eat." I remained calm and began making dinner, antipasto, and penne with red sauce. I poured one of Grandpa's favorite Chianti wines thinking about what I was going to do when I find Ed.

After dinner Mom said, "I love you, Kachada."

"I know you do, Mom. I love you." She was tired and I insisted she get some sleep. It felt good to hear those words. *I love you.* She had never spoken those words to me before.

The next morning mom went to work, a good sign she was feeling better. I got dressed and drove directly to see my boyhood friend Little. When I arrived, Little was waiting at the front door. "JT, How's your mom?" Little asked.

I walked right past him into the living room and plopped down on his worn out '50s couch. It was splattered with food stains and blunt burns. "JT." *My friends at Franklin always called me JT.* "I knew you would come by once you heard about it. It was the Reagle boys. But you already figured that out," Little said. *I always called him Little. His real name was Richard.*

"As soon as mom mentioned the thick red hair," I said. The Reagle boys were always assholes, even when they were kids. And now they had the nerve to terrorize my mother. Ed, the smaller of the two, had red hair and a garbage mouth. John was an oversized oaf. Both had always been trouble. I sat on the couch and said, "Little, I need to find them." Little and I had our fair share of trouble as kids, but never anything more than hopping trains to Pittsburgh and stealing a police car. We knew better than to steal from or disrespect any family in our neighborhood.

Little was concerned about my violent reaction. My black musician friend began to turn white as he sat on the edge of his couch, muttering, "Whoa. Hey, you don't want to end up in the penitentiary, JT."

At the top of my voice, I shouted, "Where can I find the Reagle boys?"

Little tried his best to calm me down. "JT, be cool."

I snapped and held the tight curls of his black hair and screamed, "Where the fuck are they, Little?"

Little had always been easy to intimidate and cried out, "At the Kirby's Avenue bar." As I was leaving, Little shouted, "JT, don't let those two perdente get you in trouble." *Perdente, Italian for born losers.*

I sat in my car outside Kirby's Avenue Bar listening to "Cisco Kid Was A Friend Of Mine" on the radio. I slid the ivory-handled knife I took from Grandpa's office desk into my right boot, the brass knuckles from his office drawer onto my right hand. I walked to the door and imagined how it would go. *Marty, the bouncer, would be sitting on the left. He is a massive man who hates me because I tossed him out of Goldstein's Bar.* As soon as I walk in, Marty is standing right where I expected him to be. I hit him with the brass knuckles. I knocked him off his feet and left him lying on the floor with a deep gash between his eyes.

Chico knew why I was there. "JT, don't do it," he said.

I pointed to Ed and John standing at the other end of the bar and bellowed in Sicilian, "I'm going to fuck you up Ed."

Ed screamed, "Parolacce." *Fuck you in Sicilian.*

John came at me, throwing a wild punch that caught my jaw. At that moment everything went red. I was overtaken with rage. I grabbed John's arm and the knife from my boot, he reached for it, accidentally slicing off his thumb. Blood sprayed over both of us.

John doubled over, crying, clutching the empty space where his thumb once was. Ed mortified, pulled a small 22-caliber pistol from his leather jacket pocket. He fired two shots just missing me by inches. I landed a kick to his chest and watched him slump to the floor. From the back of my collar, Big John tossed me across the room and pounced his three-hundred-pound body on top of me. I fought to breathe as he repeatedly bounced my head onto the floor. His missing thumb was bleeding in my face, making it hard to see. I found his hand and jammed my finger into the empty space. He let out a scream. Ed jumped in, searching for his pistol on the floor as I kneed big John in the nuts and knocked him to my side. I took Ed's red hair and slammed his head onto the floor next to me, causing him to pass out and drop the pistol.

John struggled to get his 300-pound body up I kicked his right knee and hit him with two quick blows to his head, taking him back to the floor. I held Ed up by his hair and dragged him unconsciously across the floor to retrieve my knife, screaming, "Babbu!"

He knew what those words meant, *Sicilian for you fool.* I wanted to make sure he never spit in anyone's face again. I yanked his mouth open till I heard it snap and pulled his tongue out as far as I could and started cutting it out. Big John shook, screaming, unable to get up. The small crowd in the bar was horrified at the savage sight. They moved towards the back curious what I would do next. It was a hard crowd that had seen ugly before. Big John was lying on the floor sobbing as I tossed Ed's bloody tongue next to him. Ed remained unconscious as I dropped his head to the floor. I gave him what he deserved, a dose of Cosa Nostra justice. It was a savage act that terrified everyone in the bar. Including me.

Big John tried to wiggle away from the bloody tongue, pleading for me to leave him alone. The bar had become a bloody scene. Ed with a permanent speech impediment and Big John missing a thumb, I didn't kill them, but I made damn sure I left them marked forever.

Chico stood behind the bar, "JT, you need to leave. Now." He shook his head in disgust and screamed, "JT, leave before the cops get here." I turned to the spectators in the back and heard Chico say, "They won't be a problem, JT. Get the fuck out of here."

I left the bar and drove to the airport car return. Inside, I went to the restroom to wash up before boarding the plane. I called Mom leaving a message that I loved her and told her she wouldn't be having any more problems. I took my bag and got on the flight without any remorse flight thinking, *I did what needed to be done.*

During a layover in Madrid, I thought about what the evil Reagle boys had done to my mom and the conversation I had with Hayri. *"Those bastards took my family from me."* Maybe Hayri is hunting Shafik to revenge his family just as I did, delivering Mafia style justice to those who would dare harm my family. The Reagal boys found out just what that meant.

CHAPTER 10

September 5, 1974, Milan, Italy

The last few days had been a whirlwind of events, and they took a toll on me. After being awakened by a party in the suite next to me, I ambled over to the bar and poured water over a glass of ice. I glanced at my watch; it was 2:00 p.m. I noticed the newspaper under my door and picked it up. I realized I had been asleep two and a half days. *2,880 minutes of my life.*

The Canadian Grand Prix in Mosport Park and the U.S Grand Prix in Watkins Glen were the last two races of the season. I kept my promise to Jean-Pierre and finished the racing circuit. Jeane-Pierre handed me a six-figure check for a job well done and asked if I would cover next year's event. I graciously refused, and took the money, donating it to a cause I could relate to: St. Jude Children's Research Hospital, dedicated to ending childhood cancer.

It had been nine weeks since I'd first met the odd-looking Hayri in Zurich. Sitting in the hotel, starring at his business card, I weighed my options. *"Because I learned all about you. And we both want to find Shafik before he finds you."* Those words haunted me and I was afraid Safik would be looking for me. I dialed Hayri's number.

Hayri answered speaking German, "Hallo."

I paused, then said, "Hayri, it's Kachada. Perhaps we should meet."

Hayri's voice brightened up, "Kachada have you ever been to Paris?"

"No," I said.

"It's a city you will fall in love with and it will love you back. Can we meet at Ze Kitchen Galerie on the Seine River, across from the Cathedral of Notre Dame de Paris?" Hayri asked.

"When?" I asked.

"Wednesday, October twenty-third at 2 p.m. You will be there?" Hayri asked.

I waited thinking, *"What this could lead to."* Then I said, "I will be there."

"Kachada. It is so good to hear from you," Hayri said.

I hung up and reviewed his business card one more time, thinking, *"What do I have to lose by meeting with this strange man?"*

I arrived early to explore the local art gallery scene and booked the Le Pavillon de la Reine Hotel in Quartier Maraisin. It was close to the Musee Picasso. Art was an escape from my world. Chief Peta's wise words were always with me, *"Kachada, art is a powerful medicine."*

The city was alive with holiday decorations. Along the *rues* of Paris, the crowds walked with purpose, carrying an intoxicating energy. After my morning espresso, I listened to the sounds of taxis racing to their next fare as I walked by the Eiffel Tower looming overhead. The fresh café aromas were on every corner. As I passed by one on Rue du Temple I stopped in mid-stride. Tentatively I walked up to the street poster in front of the Modus Art Gallery as if I had just discovered a rare species. The image taunted passers-by who couldn't walk by without stopping to admire it. I mustered the courage to step closer to read the large lettered headline: *Aponi.* Then the caption below the image: *A full-blooded American Indian beauty. Painted by world-renowned artist, Comanche Chief Peta.* I stood in front of a painting by my grandpa, embraced by the historical beauty of Paris.

It had been over a year since I last saw the beautiful Aponi. The Chief's masterpiece had captured the essence of her beauty. Her Comanche headband and necklace were made up of rows of turquoise and beads strung against her flawless red skin. Her black almond-shaped eyes and long, thick black hair were accented by a white, blue, and black feather hanging from her braided hair, pointing towards her bare breasts.

"Bienvenue to the Modus Gallery," someone said.

Lost in the painting, I could only muster a smile. The lovely young woman handed me a pamphlet. "Here is a brochure of Chief Peta's works inside. The prices are listed on the back. Numbered to match the art hanging on the walls. Come in. If you have any questions, please don't hesitate to ask. My name is Elodie."

"Marsh-flower. *Elodie is French for marsh flower,*" I said after I came to my senses.

"You speak French," she said enthusiastically. And took my hand, guiding me inside like a lost child. Maybe my heart was in overdrive after seeing the beautiful portrait of Aponi, but Elodie was indeed a beautiful flower. Her tall thin frame, tan skin, and short sassy brown hair wisped over her 1950s-style black-rimmed glasses, capturing a mysteriously attractive likeness to Audrey Hepburn.

I accepted the brochure and said. "Merci."

Once inside, she ushered me past the contemporary canvases and sculptures to a wall-size printed poster of Grandpa's portrait. Next to it was his history silkscreened on the wall. It was odd for me to see the art I watched him painted on the reservation was now hanging in a Paris gallery. The same mountains and valleys were being shared with the world. Horses running wild in the canyons, pottery sitting on clear polyurethane stands with spotlights showcasing the intricate designs. Meticulously etched into clay with black and white shapes, each depicting the Comanche ancestry. I could feel his spirit standing next to me.

"Powerful, no?" Elodie said clearing her throat.

Taken by her beauty and soft voice I said, "Have you met him?"

Elodie shook her head no and said, "But the owner of the gallery has. She said he lives on a real Indian reservation somewhere in America. Maybe one day he might visit our Paris gallery."

I stared at her until her eyes began to shift awkwardly. Finally, I admitted, "He's my grandpa." I watched her eyes sparkle. "Nanisuyake," I said. "It's Comanche for beautiful," I told her. "When I first met Aponi she was a teenager. She's more beautiful than I remembered."

Elodie reached for my hand. "I would love to hear about Chief Peta over coffee. Would you join me?" I was so captivated by her I remained silent, until she whispered, "Sorry, I offended you."

"No. I would enjoy your company," I told her. Elodie's eyes smiled. She informed the other gallery hostess she was leaving to discuss art pieces with me at the Royal Turene.

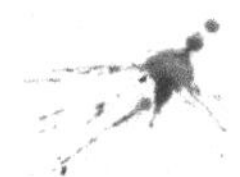

We sat in a row of blue leather seats facing the glass windows, each etched with the restaurant's name. They revealed the busy street and array of people walking behind them. The restaurant hummed with activity, creating a background for the beautiful French language.

Elodie sat next to me and ordered two lattes and a crème brûlée to share. I caught the eyes of others walking by as they tried to sneak a glimpse of her contagious beauty. Elodie, seemingly unaware of her beauty she listened, closely watching my lips as I relived my younger days with Grandpa. Her eyes sparkled every time I mentioned sitting next to Chief Peta, watching him paint. Her warm body melted into mine. We had lost track of time when she asked, "Are you in Paris alone?"

I said, "Oui, at Le Pavillon de la Reine."

"Would you like company?" she asked. The intensity of my eyes frightened most people, but not Elodie.

Then I asked, "the gallery?"

She rubbed her shoulder into mine and said, "Mais c'est Paris." *But this is Paris.*

The next few days defined Paris as the *city of love*. Captivated by Elodie's energy and love for art, I found it impossible to take my eyes off of her. Sitting innocently on the bed in her tiny white cotton panties and t-shirt, with messy black hair and black glasses, she didn't care one bit about how she looked. Her tall frame and olive skin formed the perfect composition of Parisian beauty. "Kachada, here are the galleries and museums we should go to," Elodie said holding a map of Paris, London, Madrid, and Bucharest and laying it folded-out across the bed. "We can fly to any one of these and be back by the end of the day. Does that sound good to you, Kachada?"

"It sounds perfect," I said. We flew first to Bucharest, stopping along the way at the Artist Café for a light fare of lattes and a cucumber sorbet.

When we arrived at the Rotenberg, Elodie introduced me to artists I had never heard of. "This is Alexandru Nestor. His work is a collage of clock pieces and coins. What do you think?" Elodie asked.

I looked at her enchanting face and said, "Not interested in anything that is built around time." Not affected by my comment, she smiled and pulled me onwards to discover the next artist.

My smile was permanent as I took in the inspiring works of art. Elodie led me through the entire gallery, filled with new names and works, explaining the history of each. She was my private tour guide to London's Imperial War Museum and the Museo del Prado in Madrid, with European art dating from the twelfth century to the early twentieth century. We didn't waste a minute enjoying the now, not concerned with what tomorrow would bring. A life I hadn't experienced since I was nineteen.

Before I knew it, it was Wednesday, and time to meet with Hayri. Elodie and I shared an authentic French kiss goodbye before returning to her gallery.

On my walk to Ze Kitchen Gallerie, the morning traffic echoed along the Boulevard Bourdon as I crossed the Seine to Qual de la Tournelle where Ze Kitchen Galerie sat nestled among quaint shops squeezed together along the narrow cobblestone street. I asked for a table for two and snuggled up to a warm glass of cognac. I turned each page of a local paper I had plucked from the quaint purple flowered wicker basket by the front door.

On my third review of the paper and my second glass of cognac, I was annoyed that Haryi had not shown, disrespecting my time. Just as I got up to leave Hayri came from nowhere, claiming a chair at my table. Frustrated, I demanded in German, "Warum hast du mich warten lassen?" *Why did you make me wait?*

Hayri looked nothing like the man I saw in Zurich. He wasn't as rumpled. His thick hair was dark brown. He was wearing a fitted blue jacket, expensive black slacks, and a studded black leather belt. It was as if a butterfly escaped from its cocoon and turned into this handsome thirty-something man. *Again he cast an unusual aura I just couldn't explain.*

Hayri said, "I was making sure you were not followed."

"Why would anyone follow me, Hayri?" I asked.

"Axel DeKlote." Before I could speak, Hayri said, "You will learn that I know everything."

"What the merde are you talking about?" I spouted.

"The Belgian who got away in Zandvoort?" said Hayri. "Axel DeKlote is a Dutch sympathizer with Shafik-al Azora. The man hunting you." Hayri said.

Who was this Hayri guy? I remained silent.

Hayri said, "Bothe Radev."

Again, I remained silent.

"The one you killed," Hayri said. Annoyed I hadn't responded he said, "Bothe Radev is also a disciple of Shafik," Then he paused. Haryi became demonstrative. "Do you think I am a fool?" Hayri said. "Do you think I just *happened* to meet you in Zurich?" There was a short intermission as he smiled, "I did my homework on your family."

Unnerved, I stood up, shocked by what he had just told me. Here is a person I didn't know yet he found a way to invade my personal life. I began to leave. Hayri reached for my arm as I pulled away. Then he opened a mystery door I never saw coming.

In a quiet tone he said, "Kachada, my father worked with the OSS in World War II and with your father, Antonio." It was as if someone had dropped a cinder block on my head. I fell back into the chair thinking *my connection to this strange man isn't just the Belgian I killed, but now my father, too*. I remained silent, as I listened to what he was saying. "My father is Thierry Thorin. My family lived in a chateau known as the House of Thorin, in . . ."

I interrupted, recalling my grandpa's conversations on his swing, "South of France."

He said. "Yes, my real name is Francisco Thorin. My father worked alongside your father during the war. Together they blew up bridges to save our family and the villagers from the Nazis. He would speak often of your father, referring to him as his brother."

Hearing him speak of my father touched me. This strange man was telling stories about my dad I had never heard before, making me proud.

Hayri went on, "I changed my name when I was a young boy, and moved out of the region after my family was killed at the restaurant. I was playing along the waterfront, feeding the ducks, when my ears rang from the blast. I rolled up into a ball, covering my head from the falling debris. I looked up and saw the faces of the killers shooting innocent bystanders lying on the ground from the blast. Faces I still see."

"They ran past me, screaming Hanni Naif. I cried, 'You killed my family.' A woman nearby who was bleeding and hugging her baby told me to never mention it or they would return to kill me. I choked with fear, not speaking a word to anyone. I was a young boy alone with no place to go until my aunt arrived and took me with her back to her family in Trabzon. I told her what I had seen and she ordered me to never speak of it. To protect me she changed my name to Hayri Sadik, adopting me as her son. Growing up, she told me stories of how my parents helped refugees targeted by the terrorists. She said they were heroes, saving many lives." Hayri paused to catch his breath. "Your father was one of those heroes to my family and the villagers. I made it my purpose to deliver justice and send those senseless killers responsible for my parent's death to hell. Some may call it revenge. I call it justice."

There was no denying that Hayri was on a mission. "Killing another man is an ugly place to live in," I told him.

He hesitated. "I told you I knew what happened in Zandvoort."

I admitted nothing and said nothing.

"After arriving in Zandvoort, I hiked along the beach to meet up with Thomas. He was one of my informers and also a victim of terrorists. When I heard a voice cry out, I ran towards it and saw you through the thick fog fighting with one of the Belgians when I heard two shots. After you left, I ran up and discovered the man lying bloodied in the sand was my friend, Thomas. There was nothing I could do for him. I had to leave him lying in that sand without a proper burial.

"I needed to know the person who tried to save my friend and prayed for Thomas. So I followed you to the hotel and approached the front desk. They told me you were Kachada Toscano." Hayri produced a crooked smile. A smile I would become all too familiar with. "I recognized your name from RACE magazine. I have always loved racing and followed the Grand Prix and enjoyed your writing style. I saw it as an excuse to meet you. Thomas was following the two Belgians, searching for information I hoped would have led me to Shafik. It appeared he knew too much."

At this point, I kept the information about the Belgian calling out Shafik's name before he died to myself, and let Hayri continue. "I did my research and discovered you were the grandson of Comanche Chief Peta, the renowned Native American artist. I became obsessed with the mystery of you. I flew to Dallas and drove to the reservation and convinced Chief Peta to talk to me. Then I made it my mission to meet with your mother."

My face had turned to stone. Hayri saw my cold look and pleaded, "After I explained how I knew about her husband, Antonio, she decided to meet with me in the hospital cafeteria. She patiently listened to me. Your mom decided she could trust me and told me about you."

"And what was that?" I asked.

"I know why you live life on the edge. How you battle the constant pain from the effects of the radiation." I remained quiet as he talked on. "There is an ugly side to this world. The side you saw killing Thomas. Because of your heroic attempt to save Thomas, this has brought you to that evil world. Because of Axel DeKlote, the Belgian that got away, Shafik is now, as you know, hunting you."

I protested, "Axel, or whatever his fucking name was, has no idea who I am.

"If I know he knows," Hayri said.

"Don't forget the Esmeralda," Hayri reminded me.

The only thing that made sense was to remain silent.

"The man they threw overboard, the Czechoslovakian ambassador. Where you first met them. Like it or not, you are someone they think is their enemy. Become the hunter, and join me. Help me put them where they belong: in hell." Hayri leaned closer, "Kachada, we are fighting the same evil people your father and mine fought together."

Hayri saw my internal struggle and reached into this shirt pocket. He handed me a folded piece of yellow paper torn from a college-ruled writing pad. I didn't open it. I just looked at him holding an ugly secret I didn't want to know. Hayri knew I was not ready and said, "I will call you later to see if you would like to continue this conversation."

I was still curious about his comment concerning my writing. "You didn't explain why you're interested in my writing."

He flashed that crooked smile. "After you read the note, and if you choose to meet, I will explain why your writing would be important to both of us."

Once inside my hotel room, I stripped to my underwear and lit a blunt to take the edge off the emotionally draining day. My mind was whirling with thoughts and what ifs.

Then I heard a voice, "Kachada rejoins moi."

I choked, swallowing the smoke from my blunt. Elodie was lying naked in the bed. I didn't care how she got there. I tossed my joint into a glass vase and joined her.

"Bonjour." Elodie woke me with a morning kiss. I reached up and ran my fingers through her thick sassy hair. She gave me a quick kiss and got up to finish dressing. She shook her hair into place, then blew me a kiss and left.

I went to my leather jacket lying on the floor and reached into the inside breast pocket. Unfolding the paper Hayri gave me, I dropped the jacket back to the floor. I held the note thinking, *what does this mean if I read it?* I opened it.

> PLO: Leonardo da Vinci-Fiu-micino International Airport in Rome. December 1973. 34 people killed.
>
> Unknown: LaGuardia Airport Bombing December 29. 1963. 11 killed, 75 wounded.

The note was a list of targets connected to terrorist bombings. I carefully started to read them when the phone rang. I picked it up and heard, "Hello." It was Hayri. "Have you read the note?" he asked.

Looking at it, I said, "I started to."

"Should we meet?" Hayri asked. The silent response caused Haryi to say, "Kachada, the list is just one raindrop of a violent storm."

Hayri understood the value of a powerful metaphor. Holding the list in my hand, I knew the impact of what he was asking of me. My life would never be the same. "Oui," I said.

I could hear Hayri's voice brighten, "Bien, *good,* my friend. Meet me at the corner of Rue de Clery and Rue Montmartre at 10:00 tomorrow morning."

My twenty-minute morning walk ended at an elegantly remodeled building looking to be hundreds of years old. Above me was a two-story neon sign hanging over the entrance. The white neon letters were framed within a bright red square spelling PEUR DE RIEN, *French for fear nothing,* above a glass entrance reminding me of Times Square.

Through the glass doors, I was confronted by a series of life-size magazine covers. They were placed throughout the lobby, creating a maze of fashion photography presenting a dramatic impression.

"What do you think?" I was surprised to find Hayri standing behind me.

"Why choose a place like this to meet?" I asked.

By now I should have known to expect the unexpected with Hayri. He handed me a badge with my name on it, *Kachada Toscano Journaliste, PEUR DE RIEN.* "Are you telling me all this is yours?" I said, holding the badge. *A princess must have kissed the shabby man I met in Zurich, turning him into some sort of royalty.*

"Follow me," he said. His footsteps echoed along the glossy black marble floor. At first, I didn't move. I waited to remind him that I made my own decisions. He looked my way, waving me on. I decided to join him and weaved my way through the fashionable crowd. Hayri stood before a life-size silver print of the pop singer Carly Simon.

"What now?" I asked as I stared at the glamorous image of Carly.

Hayri turned and looked into Carly's eyes. Suddenly a hidden door opened. *Hayri the magician*. We stepped into an elevator that whisked us to the top floor, opening onto a high-tech war room overlooking the streets of Paris.

Eyes followed me, making me uncomfortable. I joined Hayri around a glass table featuring a hologram of Central Asia. The others in the room who were watching me gathered around. Hayri introduced me to a potpourri of faces. "This is Kachada Toscano, the grandson of Comanche Chief Peta."

I whispered, "What do they know?"

"Those standing here with me are all survivors," Hayri said. And turned to a wall-size screen projecting faces with a dossier of names responsible for so many ruthless killings and terrorist attacks.

"This is Abu Naif, he's been on the list since 1972. Abu broke away from the PLO and formed the Abu Naif Organization, known as ANO. He's responsible for ordering attacks in over ten countries and killing over two hundred innocent people." Hayri turned to me and said, "He is also the son of Hanni Naif, who is responsible for killing my family."

Okay, Hayri made his point. The apple didn't fall far from the tree.

Hayri said, "He is our target." Hayri then brought up the headshot of the Belgian I had killed. "This is Bothe Radev a disciple of Shafik and part of Abu Naif Organization." Hayri again turned to me. "Kachada killed Bothe in Zandvoort." The unnamed faces gave a subtle grin. Hayri then pointed to the next mug shot, "This is Axel DeKlote, also a Belgian and a disciple of Shafik. He escaped Kachada in Zandvoort. That means Kachada is now on Shafik's list. And we know what that means. Abu is our target and on the most wanted lists of the CIA, Interpol—and the Mossad," Hayri said.

I asked, "Then why not let them kill him?"

Hayri glanced around the table. "And that may happen. But he has managed to elude them, never having to pay for the crimes he, his father, and his father's father committed. For decades his family has preached to their disciples in the name of Allah the evil of those not Muslim. He has convinced them to commit acts of terror against innocent people." Hayri walked up to the large image of Abu. "While the CIA, MI5 and the others have to play politics, we don't." Haryi glanced my way, "Unlike the others hunting him, we answer to no one. Like the *lord of the plains,* we strike swiftly leaving no survivors."

I appreciated the knowledge he had of my Comanche ancestors. "What about Shafik and Axel?" I asked.

Hayri said, "Abu will bring us closer to them."

I didn't like his answer. With only 43,800 minutes left, I was standing among a group of dedicated rogue assassins asking me to join their cause. I thought, *Do I even have a choice, now that Shafik knows who I am.*

CHAPTER 11

December 15, 1974,
Paris, France

The Comanche believe, *"To survive in the beauty of nature you have to kill the ugly beasts that live within it."* Hayri was committed to finding Shafik, Axel and those like Abu. The ugly beasts that have been terrorizing the world we were living in for decades. My decision was clear.

Thanks to Hayri, I traveled throughout Europe and Central Asia with a cover as a fashion journalist, documenting the latest fashion trends from up-and-coming designers for his magazine. My visa read: Jouranaliste Kachada Toscano. PEUR DE RIEN.

Before the upcoming assignment of covering the Tel Aviv fashion show, I used my photographic memory to learn Hebrew. After the Tel Aviv show, I returned to my hotel room to find an envelope placed under my door. It was a note from Hayri attached to a one-way ticket to Beirut.

From my sixth floor view of the Mediterranean at the Phoenicia Hotel, I poured my first glass of Arak over ice: a drink indigenous to Beirut. Sitting on the balcony, I sipped the 126-proof drink as the doorbell rang.

It was Hayri. This time he looked like the person I met in Zurich. He was transformed back into the smelly, disheveled man with tea-stained teeth, wearing a gray fedora. "You forgot to shower before you left Paris?" I said.

"When I'm in this part of the world, I prefer to appear less successful and more peasant-like. It helps me to blend in," Hayri replied.

I said, "You succeeded."

Hayri noticed I was drinking an Arak. He contorted his face in disgust. "Why are you drinking such swill?" Hayri asked.

I swished the Arak around my mouth, walked over to the sink, spit it out, and tossed the rest down the drain. "It *is* swill," I said. I opened a bottle of cognac and we sat on the balcony enjoying the light breeze.

Hayri wasted no time pulling out a loose-leaf binder from his attaché and handed me a picture of Abu Naif's face attached to a dossier. "I've been tracking this animal responsible for torturing and raping political opponents and innocent captives. There are stories of him pulling their fingernails out and burning their genitals. Some of the victims saved were committed to psychiatric wards."

"Gruesome," I said.

Hayri read Abu's resume. "TWA Flight 841 crashed into the Ionian Sea after taking off from Rome. Pan Am flight 110 saw an engine separate from the wing before it spiraled into the sea. The National Transportation Safety Board determined a bomb hidden in the cargo hold area destroyed the plane. All seventy-nine passengers were killed. The plot had Abu Naif written all over it. He is aligned with Shafik, and together they planned attacks across Europe. I traced Abu from Antwerp to Ostrava to Damascus—and now to here. Abu has been seen living in a northern town near the Syrian border—in the small village of Halba. Halba is divided between the Sunni Muslims and Greek Orthodox Christians. The Muslims live in the Akkar District, home of the Sada Akkar newspaper. This area is known for aiding terrorists. It is where Abu chose to hold up just outside of Massoudieh."

I was impressed with the detailed report. "Massoudieh? How do we get there?" I asked.

"It would normally take two hours. But we will travel at night, taking back roads I have mapped out." He showed me a map and pointed. "This route will take us about five hours. Route 51M from Beirut, north though Governorate to Bcharre, Bcharre to Tannourine Road, and we'll drive along Tripoli onto the Aarida Highway to Qoubaiyat Road."

"That sounds like a beating," I confessed.

"My driver, Ihsan, will pick us up," Hayri replied.

"Kindness," I translated.

"You've been studying the language. Ihsan is also an enemy of Abu. Abu killed his brother-in-law in a local bombing. Ihsan will be here tomorrow before sunrise. I will have weapons for us once we are outside of Beirut." He paused and asked, "Do you have any second thoughts?"

"It is better to be the hunter," I answered.

Early the next morning, the landscape passed by my window as Ihsan drove us across dirt roads. We bounced like rag dolls all the way to Massoudieh. The buildings weren't as disheveled as I expected them to be, considering the many years of conflicts. The tapestry of small thatched roofs against modern buildings passing by Al-Nabk and Tripoli were not what I expected.

Four hours in, the hot bumper car was torture. It was a relief when we pulled off to the side of the road to drain all of the water I drank trying stay hydrated.

Hayri opened the plans and laid them over the rusted trunk of the car. He pointed at an area outlined in red. "We are a couple hours from Abu's location." Ihsan handed us each a prayer rug and said, "Best to blend in." We kneeled as Ihsan led us in the Dhuhu prayer.

After the prayer, we drove on for two more hours. The sun was beginning to set. We pulled onto a narrow street. Ihsan handed each of us a black onyx-handled ten-inch curved blade inside a leather quiver, called a Khanjar dagger, and a Desert Eagle.

I held the Desert Eagle and said, "The Mossad is known for this weapon."

Hayri smiled. "Yes. Today we are the Mossad. The Hezbollah are deathly afraid of the Mossad and they will be convinced they killed Abu."

The normally quiet Ihsan spoke up, "The Mossad would do it by slitting their throats, and would use the Desert Eagles only when necessary. Once you are inside you have to kill everyone."

"Why do you want them to think Mossad did it?" I asked.

Hayri said, "Abu and his organization know the CIA, MI5, and Mossad are hunting him. The one they fear most is Mossad. By making it look like the Mossad killed him, we remain anonymous. Which makes us even more dangerous."

Ihasan said, "The sun is setting."

Hayir and I made our way across the sand towards Abu's villa. I got about five yards away and fell to the ground, crawling to keep my head low. The villa was decorated with decades of war-ravaged scars. Chickens and cats ran by, undisturbed by our presence. I stood up and leaned against the wall near the back door, where two dismantled vans sat. Hayri positioned on the north side and I was on the south end, within sight of each other. Hayri held up his hand to signal when the sound of a car driving off surprised us.

We both ran to watch a VW Rabbit motoring down the road leaving a trail of dust.

"He made us?" I asked.

Hayri was obviously upset, and we scurried through the sand, back to Ihsan who sat on top of the Renault's hood, wearing his night vision goggles. Hayri impatiently growled, "Who was that?"

"Abu," Ihsan replied. I could hear the disappointment in his voice.

"Was he alone?" Hayri barked.

Ihsan, upset, jumped from the car, swearing in Arabic. "Yes." He began to pace like an angry dog.

"Did he make us?" I asked.

Ihsan still pacing. "No. He wasn't driving like someone trying to get away."

"Shouldn't we follow him?" I shouted back.

"Why didn't you shoot him?" Hayri challenged Ihsan.

"How? It was dark and the noise would have blown our cover as the Mossad," Ihsan said pushing his chest into Hayri.

I grabbed Ihsan's keffiyeh and pulled him back. Ihsan threw his fist at me, knocking me to the ground. Then he drew his dagger, putting it to my throat.

"Stop," shouted Hayri.

Ihsan got back up and muttered curse words and walked away.

Seething, I screamed, "He must have warned Abu."

Hayri held me and said, "You are wrong."

Ihsan paced and screamed, "I will find him."

Haryi consoled Ihsan and said, "Ihsan will drop us at Al'Abdah and get back to us in the morning." Hayri glanced towards me. "Al'Abdah is just twenty minutes south of here, towards Tripoli. It is a small village on the sea where we can rest until Ihsan finds Abu."

I told Hayri, "I don't trust him."

But Hayri became angry and said, "I trust him with my life, enough of this. Perhaps you don't belong after all."

No one spoke during the hot bumpy ride. The frustration and tension were obvious. When we arrived at a small, two-story farmhouse on a back road, we were tired from the anxiety of not knowing where Abu was, and from the tension during the ride. The sound of boarded horses and farm animals surrounded us as we pulled into the open barn. Hayri put our weapons into a wooden tool chest as Ihsan drove off. I followed Hayri to the side door of the farmhouse and was greeted by a short, round forty-something woman wearing a traditional head wrap and long-robe as a dress.

Hayri and the woman kissed like cousins. "You must be hungry, sit down—have some dolmas and hummus," suggested the kind woman. To my surprise, her face was soft and showed no signs of wrinkles. Her eyes were green. Not what I would have expected in this part of the world.

Hayri said, "This is my cousin Aslan's wife, Asma. It means *precious* in Arabic, and she is precious to me." The woman nodded and went about the business of cooking. "Aslan, Asma's husband, and my cousin were killed along with twenty-nine other passengers on Pan Am flight 110 in December of 1973 by Abu's followers. They threw phosphorus bombs aboard the plane as it prepared for departure, destroying the entire plane with everyone on it." He reminded me why we were chasing Abu.

I asked with my mouth full of hummus, "What do we do while we wait for Ihsan to return?"

Hayri was gobbling up yabra, *stuffed grape leaves*. "We go to bed and hope that by tomorrow Ihsan has located Abu. If not, we retreat to Paris and regroup."

"Retreat. I don't like that word or the idea," I said gritting my teeth.

"Nor do I," Hayri said.

Ihsan returned early the next morning with more frustrating news. He could not locate Abu. We drove four hours in the hot Renault back to Beirut. I checked back into the Phoenicia Hotel and flopped onto the king size soft bed made of duck down. I immediately fell asleep while still wearing the dusty, sweaty kaftan.

Early the next morning I was running on the Eddeh Sands beach. I was angry thinking about Ihsan losing our target, Abu. I didn't trust him regardless of what Hayri said. Around me, the citizens of Beirut were starting their day, drowning out the sounds of the waves washing onto the beach.

The modern war-torn city and the people carried on, ignoring the daily dangers that were trying to swallow their lives. Signs of Russian money and mobsters had infiltrated businesses, including the nightclub scene. They managed to get their hands into the ugly underbelly of drug trafficking and white slavery.

Beirut had the reputation of being the playground of Central Asia. I decided to find out for myself if it was true. The hotel concierge recommended the Skybar, but warned me one night at the club would cost me thousands of dollars. I took the concierge's recommendation and arrived with plenty of cash. It was 1:00 am and the club was exploding with dancers on stage and on the tables. Once inside the old building, it was as modern as you would find in an exclusive Manhattan club. The pounding music set the pace for the mesmerizing light show.

Two bouncers who greeted me put their hands over my chest and down my pants before they gave me the approval to enter the club. I walked inside and immediately two tall and exotic young Russian girls dressed in short dresses and very high heels approached me. They were stunningly beautiful. One had long blonde hair and the other short brown hair. They showed off the pointed breasts poking into their translucent dresses.

The blonde spoke French and said, "I am Nonna and this is Oksana. We will escort you to your table." I gladly accepted. Nonna ordered a bottle of expensive Vodka and made herself comfortable on my lap. "What is your name?" Nonna asked. I wasn't sure if I should say, so I just smiled.

"Ah, a mystery man. We like mysterious men. Don't we Oksana?" Nonna said. Oksana was the taller of the two and she joined Nonna and put one long leg on either side of me, giving a clear view of her Brazilian cut resting on my lap. Nonna melted into my side, stroking Oksana's short thick hair. Then Oksana slid her hands under my shirt and said, "Before the night is over, there will be no more mysteries."

I tilted my head back and noticed the glass railing above us. It was the namesake of the Skybar. After an hour of drinking vodka, I reconnected to the Skybar above us, startled by what I saw. A man who resembled Abu was above me and I sat up, startling Nonna and Oksana. I tried to get a better look but the flashing rainbow-colored strobe lights made it impossible. I had to find my way to the Skybar and see if it was Abu that I had seen. If so, this time I couldn't let him escape.

Nonna began to tickle my ear with her tongue, I pulled back to return the favor and whispered, "Nonna, is there a private room?"

As Oksana played with Nonna's breasts she said, "It will be very expensive."

She knew she had me excited. "Nothing is too expensive," I replied. She gave me a lusty smile and whispered in Oskana's ear.

They kissed each other and asked me, "What would you like?"

I didn't know what to say, so I slipped my hand down her sheer dress over her pointed nipples and said, "Everything."

Oksana left, returning with a polite, well-dressed Lebanese man. Speaking French he said, "I am Sahi. I understand you would like to be alone with our beautiful Nonna and Oksana. If you like, I can take you to a private place where you will not be disturbed. But I warn you, it is very expensive."

It worked. "I would like that," I said kissing Nonna.

Sahi gave me his concierge smile. "My pleasure, follow me." I stood up and we followed Sahi to the glass elevator, which took us up to the Skybar. Walking along the glass railing, I glanced below at the crowd pulsing under flashing strobe lights like a scene from *Dante's Inferno.*

I scanned the layout, passing by the row of private rooms. Each one had sheer gauze curtains hanging from ceiling-to-floor revealing the provocative silhouettes of the intimate playgrounds. I counted six rooms, not including the one Sahi gestured for us to enter.

Sahi said, "Everything you need is here, Mr. Toscano. If not, please use the phone to call for any service you wish." He held his hand out and said, "That will be six thousand U.S. dollars." I handed him seven thousand, knowing he was expecting a tip. He took the time to count it and reminded me, "You are welcome to the Skybar anytime, Mr. Toscano." Then Sahi shouted to Nonna and Oksana, "Take care of Mr. Toscano's needs."

Nonna slipped out of her minidress and was wearing her black heels said, "So you do have a name, Mr. Toscano."

Oksana spread herself across the soft white king-size bed. Nonna pressed her naked body into mine, slipping her hand into my pants. "Don't worry, he is in good hands."

Sahi watched Nonna and mumbled as he left the room.

Indeed I was in good hands. Oksana joined Nonna. Their hands were like Picasso's brushes redefining the norm with each movement they took my body on in this new journey. After an hour of exploring our fantasies, I opened another bottle of champagne. Exhausted from the psychedelic experience, I needed to get back to why I was here. Nonna and Oksana had been drinking Dom and took turns licking the expensive bubbly from their body parts. Eventually, they passed out from the coke, vodka, champagne and exotic sex.

Covered in oil and wet from sweat, I managed to wiggle from between them without waking either one. I pushed my shoulder-length hair onto my back and walked along to the railing, drinking from a bottle of Dom observing the dancing crowd below. I sensed an uneasy presence behind me and carefully turned to find Abu looking at me. He was shirtless, wearing only a baggy pair of silk pants. *The man we followed from Massaoudieh to Beirut was now standing less than two feet away.* I began plotting what I could do and how I would do it.

"I like the tattoo," he said, speaking French. His deep voice surprised me.

"It is called the Zia Sun," I said in French.

"What is the Zia Sun?" Abu asked.

"A Native American Indian symbol that signifies rebirth," I said. Abu just smiled. I said, "I came across a Native American tattoo artist in Vegas. I liked the design."

"So you are French?" Abu asked.

"No, I'm Sicilian."

He said, "You sound French wearing a tattoo of a Native American, but now you say you are a blonde Sicilian?" He laughed. "I am Hanni. And you are?"

When he said, Hanni, I began thinking *of Hayri telling me Abu was the son of Hanni. He was using his murdering father's name.* "I am Kachada," I said.

"Kachada. Interesting name. What does it mean?" Abu asked.

"Comanche for white man," I said.

He shook his head, "Now you have a Comanche name." He looked into my room. "Your whores are no longer useful to you."

I tried to be coy. "They did their best."

He surprised me by asking, "Join me?" He walked towards his VIP room while I remained still. Abu turned and said, "Kachada, nothing to worry about. I like women." I nodded and followed him to his room.

Abu shouted, "Whores, leave us." The girls ran half-naked out of the room carrying the rest of their clothes. "There is nothing more they can do for me." He laughed and held up a small mirror with two lines of coke. He waited for a moment. When I didn't accept he smiled and snorted one of the two lines. I picked up the tiny silver tube and snorted the remaining line thinking, *this could be the only chance I will have to kill him.*

"Tell me about yourself, Kachada?" Abu asked relaxing against the headboard.

"I'm a fashion writer," I said.

"In Beirut?" Abu asked.

"No, a magazine in Paris. I was covering a show in Tel Aviv and heard about the exotic nightlife of Beirut. So I decided to find out for myself," I told him.

"I hope Beirut is treating you well…" Abu's voice started warbling and my head began to spin.

My vision became blurred, as I saw an image enter his room, and Abu walked away.

Fuck I thought as my world began to turn black.

My head was pounding as if I had a migraine. I felt dirt going into my ears and sensed I was moving. I struggled to open my eyes, seeing only blurred shapes and sounds I couldn't process. My body was like a rag doll being dragged through sand. A large shape in front of me was holding my legs, pulling me and then I stopped. I heard a familiar voice speaking Arabic. I could only move my eyes but the rest of my body was numb. "This is a good place," the voice said.

I worked to focus and saw Ihsan standing at my feet. *That fucker. Just as I thought, he did warn Abu that night.* Confused, I could hear the sound of waves. Ihsan picked up my legs again and started pulling me closer to the smell of salt water. My legs dropped to the sand with a hard thud.

Another voice spoke out, "Is he awake?" the voice asked.

I saw a pair of black shoes and looked up, trying to put the image into focus. Then the man kneeled revealing his face. Sahi, I *screamed,* but no one could hear me. I had no control over any of my other senses. Sahi puts his hand on my face and lifted my eyelids wider to look into my eyes. "Yes," he said. He stood up, leaving only his shoes, and walked out of my limited sight line. My head was swirling making me nauseous.

Then a warbled voice spoke, saying, "You snorted a drug that made your body temporarily paralyzed. I know you can hear me. Abu asked me to give you this." I could only see sandals filled with dirty cracked toes and uncut nails and a tip of a sword lifted out of my sight and felt a sensation along my side. I looked down and saw blood dripping onto the sand from my right side. My body was so numb I couldn't feel it being sliced open. Then the person kneeled down to look directly into my face. It was Axel DeKlote, the Belgian who got away in Zandvoort. I struggled to reach up and grab him, *but nothing moved.* He leaned into my ear and said, "This one is for Radev, you bastard." He stood up and I heard a whoosh and sensed dripping from my other side.

The image of Axel's filthy feet moved out of sight replaced by a much larger sandal with crusty, gnarled, ugly toes. I started to move and heard the waves growing louder. My legs dropped into water as I saw an image of a large man walk towards me. He leaned into my eyesight, filling my entire view. It was Ihsan. He held a handful of my hair and started to pull me into the cold water. He pushed me further out with salt water lapping against the open wounds. It felt like someone was holding a hot iron to my sides. I faintly heard Ihsan wade back towards the beach as my mind became overrun with pain. Ihsan left me in the Mediterranean bobbing like a bleeding buoy.

Above the sound of the waves and through the burning pain I heard Ihsan's heavy voice say, "It won't be long before the sharks find him."

Senator Rubin interrupted, "Mr. Toscano. Obviously, you survived, because you are here. But how?"

"I was just as surprised as you, Senator. But before I go there I have to use the head," I said.

Senator Cornwall, spoke up, "Yes, of course. I think we could all use a personal break."

Jon showed me the way to one of the many restrooms and I shut the door. The room was as big as my bedroom. Gold faucets with framed Bierstadtand and Moran paintings hung on the walls. The wall-sized mirror was framed by wood-carved images of cowboys herding cattle. I reached for my friend and took a much-needed snort and returned to the meeting room where the Senators were waiting.

Senator Linkletter said, "Whenever you would like to continue."

"Yes of course," I said.

CHAPTER 12

January 2, 1975, Paris, France

The sound of rhythmic humming and the sensation of air swishing over me greeted me as I opened my eyes, blinking away the loose membranes, revealing a spinning ceiling fan with blades shaped like elephant ears. Was I alive? I lay still, wondering how I got from the salty waters of the Mediterranean Sea to the soft comfort of a bed. Still not sure if I was alive, I hesitated and then tentatively looked down and saw I was covered in soft white silk. I began to feel the cool sensation of a silk-covered soft pillow. Blinking from the sun rays filtering through sheer drapes blowing from left to right, I turned my head, resting deeper into the comforting pillow, and *pow*. Elodie was lying next to me. I tried to sit up and fell back, waking the *Sleeping Beauty* image.

"Kachada. You're awake?" She screamed pressing her face into mine, crying and kissing me, repeating my name. "Kachada. Kachada?" Hearing her call my name in her French accent was the closest to heaven I would ever find myself. If I believed there was such a place.

I managed to spit out, "Elodie, what day is it?"

She flashed me her big white smile saying. "It is January second."

I turned back to the elephant ear fan above me and began counting in my head, *1,052,640 minutes minus 1,051,200 minutes*. "1,440 minutes after." I let out a pathetic laugh.

Elodie looked worried. "What is it?" she asked.

I could only provide a half chuckle. "1,440 minutes after my expiration date." *It had been twenty days since I was left for shark food. Dr. Myers' prognosis would have come true if the sharks had found me.* I again expressed a weird laugh. "Yet here I am, still alive. How?" I asked.

Elodie was confused. She ran to the phone, wearing only a white t-shirt and white panties, calling out, "Hayri, he's awake. Yes, he is talking. I will."

I lay still, listening to her soft voice and fell back to sleep thinking about those *1,440 minutes.*

The sound of honking cabs brought me back to life. I forced myself to sit up and rubbed my eyes. This time Hayri and Elodie were sitting on the balcony, framed by the moonlight, sipping a drink. I started to stand up when Hayri made a dash for me, screaming, "Kachada!" He got to me before I fell.

"Hayri my friend. You have no idea how happy I am to see which face you have decided to wear today," I said sarcastically.

"Can you walk?" he asked. He helped me back up. I took a step, feeling a sharp pain on my sides. I looked down and there were two long scars on each side of my body, going from my chest to my waist. "Yes, they left you with a memory," Hayri said.

"Bastards," I replied.

Hayri helped me to the balcony and poured me a Remy from a Louis XII Magnum setting on the small table next to him. "Hayri, how did you know about Elodie?" I asked.

He took a sip. "I told you when we first met. I know everything. Now how do you feel?" Hayri asked.

"Like a fillet," I confessed.

Hayri smiled. "Good. That means your feeling is coming back. At least they didn't debone you," Hayri said with a slight laugh. I tried to laugh but it was too painful. Hayri said, "So you are 1,440 minutes older than expected. Doctor Myers would be proud."

I muttered, "Perhaps not." I changed the subject. "Now tell me how I got here?"

Haryi set his drink down. "Ihsan called me."

"I told you Ihsan couldn't be trusted. Hayri, he was the one pulling me into the Mediterranean leaving me as shark bait."

Hayri said, "I know. He told me."

"What do you mean he told you?" I shouted, feeling the pain of my wounds.

"Kachada, relax, you don't want to reopen those wounds." Hayri then said, "Ihsan pretended to work with Abu. He befriended him as a driver when he returned to Beirut, and he uses his friend, Sahi, to filter information on to me."

"Why didn't Ihsan kill Abu?" I asked.

"He is never alone." Hayri replied.

"He left with the others while I was bobbing for the sharks," I exclaimed.

"After they left, he circled back and pulled you from the sea. He knew sharks would not come around 'til the sun started to rise. He put you in his van and drove you to a doctor, who cleaned your wounds. When I arrived, I took you with me to Paris on my private jet," Hayri explained.

"You have a private jet?" I asked.

Hayri gave me that crooked smile. "After all of this, you ask me about my private jet."

I listened to Hayri, thinking *how much I have come to love this strange man.* "Haryi, I had Abu alone. Now he's still alive."

Hayri said, "He knew who you were. You took a risk and now you are in a very dangerous place. He knows your face."

"Do you have any idea where he is?" I asked. Hayri picked up his cognac taking a sip. I repeated, asking, "Hayri, do you know?"

Hayri puts his cognac down before looking at me. "I do, or should I say, *I think* I do. As you have found out, he's a slippery bastard."

I persisted, "Where do you *think* he is?"

Hayri surprised by me saying, "When you are healed." I begged for an answer but he refused. "No. You're no good to me unless you're ready. I don't need another life-saving episode and neither do you."

"Hayri, Axel DeKlote was the one who sliced me."

Hayri looked surprised. "I told you we would find them hunting Abu. It confirms my suspicion. You were on their list. You need to heal. Then we go hunting. Use this time to take in a few museums with Elodie. Then I will return to have this discussion." Hayri left us the expensive bottle of cognac.

"Aren't you forgetting something?" I asked holding the cognac.

"No, it's good pain medicine." Hayri walked out of the suite.

In the meantime, Elodie and I revived our museum list from Lisbon to Budapest. After one of the many trips, I returned to the hotel and the woman at the front desk handed me an oversized envelope. I opened it and found tickets to Barcelona with instructions from Hayri to follow a high-profile fashion show sponsored by OOko Clothing. I knew he found Abu.

In Barcelona, I visited the Artesvistas Gallery, considered the birthplace of Miro. Miro's sketches, paintings, and sculptures were a rare treat. I ended my tour at the Tapestry of the Fundacio and walked into the bookstore browsing the magazine racks.

Then I came face to face with a wall of Aponis. Her face was on all the rows of magazine covers. The headline in Spanish read:

> *"The world's next supermodel: Aponi."*

The pages were sprinkled with images of her wearing different designers' fashions, featuring several of Chief Peta's headbands and jewelry. The magnificent images supported the prediction that Aponi's unique Native American look would make her the most influential model of the next decade. *I could still see her making tacos.* I couldn't take my eyes off of her then and found it impossible now. My heart picked up a few beats looking at the covers. I thought, *Two years have passed by since I last saw her. I realized how I needed to visit Mount Pinchot overlooking the valley on the reservation. It was how I reconnected with my ancestry.*

I pulled myself from the magazines and left the bookstore. "Aponi is stunning, you must be proud." Hayri had come from nowhere once again to surprise me.

"Do you ever make a normal entrance?" I asked in frustration.

Hayri said, "No. We found Abu, and you won't believe where."

"Where?" I begged.

"He has been seen going in and out of the Pueblos," he said.

I gave him a cold stare. "The Pueblos. Are you sure it's him? What about Shafik and Axel?"

Haryi saw I was distraught over the idea of him on sacred Native American soil. "Not sure they have any idea who he is or why he is there. But my resources assure me it's him." He handed me a ticket to Dallas and said. "I booked you into the Adolphus Hotel. There is a fashion show at the Convention Center in Dallas in the next two weeks, just a mile from the hotel. He was spotted at a Pueblo just twenty-five miles northwest of Albuquerque, a nine-hour drive from Dallas."

I repeated, "Shafik and Axel?"

"After Beirut, I am confident they are working with Abu. Find Abu, and we eventually find Shafik," Hayri said. Then he left as quickly as he had appeared.

The next day I boarded Iberia Airlines filled with anxiety, thinking *Abu had the audacity to hide out on sacred Indian land.* It had been three months since my episode in Beirut. I had Abu's dossier, noting one surprise, his Special Forces training during the late 60s. I looked forward to finding him and repaying him for the scars he left me.

After my early morning run, I showered and had a craving for Primo's Grilled Beef Fajitas and a Margarita. After my Tex-Mex fix, I returned to the hotel and rented a red Mercedes 450 SL convertible, making my drive to Lawton more fun. The delivery took longer than planned, so I stayed another night and visited the nightspots recommend by the local *D Magazine*.

Dallas was as I remembered—a dynamic young city filled with energy, nightlife, and beautiful women. I started my night at the new Stark Club, named after the famous designer Phillip Stark, and ended it at the steamy Rio Room, where I had what they called in Texas "a large time." I met up with two-film reps. Lisa, a tall blonde emitted the sweet scent of coconut oil, and Heather, her redheaded girlfriend carried the scent of Ouzo liquor. We drank and danced until early morning, moving the party to my hotel room. The last thing I remembered was Lisa oiling Heather with coconut oil. I woke up to a dry mouth needing a drink. I opened a bottle of water and noticed the two bodies of flesh were entangled like licorice twists. After a shower, I took my duffle bag and left the two sleeping beauties and drove to the reservation with a morning Bloody Mary in hand.

I arrived at Grandpa's and noticed his favorite spot on the glider was empty. I surprised him when I walked inside and saw him making his favorite Indian tacos.

"Kachada," Chief Peta said. I gave him a loving hug. "Just in time for lunch," he said and handed me a freshly made taco. I put a splash of hot sauce on it. He said, "I see you have picked up more white man habits?"

I laughed, holding up the Tabasco Sauce from his table and said, "As you have."

"Kachada, it's been too long," he said.

"Yes, it has. Any new paintings?" I asked.

Chief Peta tilted his head saying, "My hands are not as strong or as steady." He held up his hands showing me how they quiver. The sight of it made me sad. He moved slower, but in my mind he would always be the strong Chief sitting tall atop his silver stallion, silhouetted by the sun. At that moment, in walked the beautiful Aponi. My eyes fixated on her.

"So that red Mercedes belongs to you?" she asked.

I couldn't make my mouth move; her beauty made me tongue-tied. I just nodded yes. She walked over and asked, "Have you forgotten how to speak Comanche?"

Trying to recover, I said, "No—I am just honored to see the *Elle cover* model standing in front of my eyes."

"I'm flattered you noticed," Aponi said. Then she gave Chief Peta a peck on the cheek.

"Hard not to when dozens of them are staring at you from the magazine rack." I held up the magazines I bought with me from Barcelona. I gave one to the Chief. He stared at it and started to flip through the pages.

The Chief looked up and asked, "Aponi, would you walk me to my studio?"

Aponi started walking with him. I got to my feet to help when she winked, signaling me to stay.

Ten minutes later Aponi returned. "Kachada, I had no idea you were coming home."

"I am in Dallas to cover a fashion show at the Convention Center," I said.

She smiled and gave me a slight model strut. "I'm the featured model for a new line in that show."

Feeling coy I said, "Aponi. Look at you now."

Aponi confessed as if she had to apologize for being so beautiful, "The high profile is good for our people. I like promoting the Indian Nation."

"The Chief's paintings and now your beauty. Brings honor to the entire Indian Nation," I said.

She changed the subject. "We need to talk about the Chief." Her tone turned serious.

"Why?" I asked.

She walked up to me and said, "His days are coming to an end. We need to spend as much time with him as possible."

I heard her but her beauty overtook the conversation.

Aponi asked. "Kachada, Are you okay? Do you need to sit down?" I tried to hold back my feelings, but I couldn't. Delicately I kissed her.

Aponi pulled back. Then she puts her long soft hands on my face and pulled me into her. She held my blonde hair and forced a wild kiss. My heart was pumping as I slipped my hands under her shirt. She slipped her top over her head, just as I said, "Stop. Aponi, I'm sorry."

She stepped out of her jeans wearing nothing but naked red skin and long black hair. Her breasts were perfectly shaped as she took a step towards me. She pressed her hand under my t-shirt and then slid her hands down into my pants. I couldn't talk, let alone breathe. At that moment I knew we would never be the same.

The day turned into evening and Aponi was dressed, preparing dinner for the chief. I picked up my clothes and got dressed, as I admired every Comanche inch of her. Soon after, the Chief arrived with the help of Kele.

Kele sensed our connection. He looked at Aponi and said, "My friend Kachada!"

Aponi's eyes glanced my way and she made an awkward offer, "Kele, stay for dinner?" she asked.

Kele said, "No thank you, Aponi." And then he asked, "Kachada, join me for a drink at the community center later?"

I said, "I'll see you there." It was an uncomfortable moment.

Once Kele left, the Chief smiled. He knew. The wise old man turned to Aponi and said, "I am happy for you."

After dinner I walked into the community center where Kele ordered me a Jack Daniels on the rocks. He wasted no time. "Aponi and you are close!"

"Yes, we are," I said.

"Kachada, the ladies' man with those blond locks and soul-piercing ice-blue eyes. And don't think I didn't notice the red convertible," Kele said with a sharp tone.

"I don't want this to come between us," I said.

Kele held my shoulders with both hands and said, "Nothing could come between us.

Yes, I'm jealous — and I'm also happy she chose you over me and not some rich white man while traveling the world as a supermodel."

"Kele, I am Kachada - *white man*," I said.

He laughed. "You're Kachada, my Comanche brother." He raised a shot of Jack Daniels. "To my Comanche brother." He noticed me staring at the bear scars on his arms and face that had become a permanent part of him.

"When I saw the brave galloping into the village holding your bloody body laying over his horse, I prayed you would survive. Look at you now, the Tribal Police Chief and a powerful warrior," I said.

Kele squeezed my shoulders and said, "The bear scars across my face and arms remind me every day what it means to be a proud Comanche warrior."

"Aponi and I leave Saturday for Dallas. But my heart is heavy seeing the chief has become too old to paint. I fear his days are not long. The time is near when Chief Peta names you Chief of our tribe," I said.

"We all feel like his sons and daughters—I promise to watch after him like a son until that time comes," Kele said.

The next morning Aponi and I drove to Dallas. When I returned to the hotel, I opened the door and there were Lisa and Heather. Both were still half-naked, lying on the bed, smelling of coconut oil, just as I left them two days ago.

Startled, Lisa jumped out of bed. "You're Aponi," she squealed. "You know Kachada?" she asked as Lisa ran over to Aponi with her bouncing coconut-oiled bare breasts.

Aponi stood still. "Kachada and I have known each other since I was a young girl," she said, staring at Lisa's breasts.

Lisa turned and ran to Heather pulling her out of bed, hissing, "Let's go." The half-naked girls took their clothes and ran out the door giggling, leaving behind the scent of coconut oil.

Aponi walked over to the bed and said, "You've been busy." Unsure of what to say I said nothing. She looked over at me and pulled the oil-stained sheets from the bed and took off her clothes. She walked over and put her arms around me whispering in my ear, "A Comanche warrior should never be alone." We fell onto the bed, reclaiming last night's passion.

Morning arrived and I told Aponi I was driving to the Pueblo art festival in New Mexico and would be back to cover the fashion show. Aponi left early to rehearse and be fitted.

Festival signs were posted along the highway where I took exit NM 259 off I-25. I followed the dirt road to a small adobe building, passing a washed-out sign that read, The Tribal Police.

I parked the red Mercedes 450 SL in the dirt lot near the sales tents already hosting a growing festival crowd. I found it interesting watching the first timers visiting. Their faces were wide-eyed as they expected to see a lifestyle of bright colors they had seen on canvases, intricate designs of pottery and the image seen in the craftsmanship of their jewelry. Instead, they found themselves walking past a landscape of poverty where makeshift repairs, uncoordinated color schemes, dirt streets and adobe homes in need of repair welcoming them to the festival.

After entertaining myself watching the newbies entering the festival entrance, I looked towards the community center next to the village market. A couple of young braves were standing on the porch, leaning against the posts in front of unmatched chairs smoking Native brand cigarettes. They were admiring my red Mercedes.

I got out the rental car to enter the festival and casually snoop around for any signs of Abu. The braves on the porch kept their eyes on the red Mercedes. My first stop was the taco stand where I ordered an Indian taco and lemonade. The sun pushed the temperature past ninety as the Sangre de Cristo Mountains began to create a Georgia O'Keeffe color palate, turning them watermelon red. It was not hard to see why *the land of enchantment* lured artists from around the world.

Not far from the taco stand, I came upon an artist's tent displaying hand-carved buffalo bones strung on silver chains with blue garnet stones carved into the form of warhorses. They were fine examples of skilled craftsmanship. An old Indian woman, seventy or so, sat alone in the corner. "If you have any questions, let me know," the Old Indian Woman said speaking Comanche.

Hearing the Pueblo woman speak Comanche surprised me. She waited for my response. "How do you know I'm Comanche?" I asked.

The Old Indian Woman gestured, "Your earring. It was designed by Chief Peta."

I touched it. I had forgotten I was wearing it. I asked, "You know of his work?"

"The Indian Nation knows his art. How did you come to have it?" the Old Indian Woman requested.

"He's my grandfather."

Her eyes opened wider, "Chief Peta is your grandfather?" The Old Indian Woman asked.

I nodded yes. "What brings you to this pueblo? Not the art," the Old Indian Woman asked.

I told her, "I'm glad I found your tent. I've never experienced a Pueblo Reservation."

The old woman changed her focus when two young braves about sixteen or so, walked into her tent. They were the same braves I saw earlier standing on the porch. They eyed me and spoke Tanoan to the old woman. I didn't understand what they are saying, but whatever it is, they were upsetting her. She finally reached into her handmade deerskin bag and handed them a roll of bills. They walked past, turning away after they saw my ice-blue eyes piercing them as they left her tent.

The old Indian woman said in Comanche, "They are bad for the village and take from the artists to feed their ugly habits."

It made me angry. "Why don't you tell the police?" I asked.

The Old Indian Woman only shook her head, "Old men, women, and children are not strong enough to stop them. The police cannot control those snakes." She leaned closer. "No one would miss the snakes." The Old Indian Woman said looking at me.

I asked, "Why don't the men of your tribe do something?"

"They are too busy getting drunk to care." The Old Indian Woman returned her focus to the jewelry she was stringing.

Surprised by her comment, I thanked her and left to search for any signs of Abu. I was walking by the Tribal police station and hesitated, I decided to enter. An officer was sitting at his desk that had wild horses carved into the front of it. It was covered with years of coffee drips, dirt, stacks of papers, and topped with an empty nameplate as if to disregard the masterpiece he was using as a desk.

The officer looked up from his magazine and saw a white-skinned blonde person and demanded, "What are you doing in here?" He seemed upset I had walked into his office.

"I'm sorry officer, but two young braves were giving an old Indian woman problems at her tent," I said.

The officer turned away, shaking his broad worn red face. "I'll look into it," he said returning his attention back the *Gun World* magazine. He didn't ask which tent. I knew nothing would come of it. So I left.

Walking out of the station, I saw the two young braves, once again, standing up against the posts of the community center. I got into the red Mercedes and revved the engine. I thought they might like the sound of it and follow me to steal it. It was common on the reservation to steal cars and strip them down to sell the parts for drugs and alcohol. I blasted out "Lyin' Eyes" before I drove off as they watched me.

At the old woman's tent, I recalled one of them had a tattoo on his face in the shape of a teardrop, close to his right eye. I recognized it as a Mexican gang tattoo known to collaborate with outlaws outside the reservation. I had dealt with this group while working at Goldstein's Bar. The tattoo led me to believe they could be connected to Abu's whereabouts. I drove back to the hotel, knowing they might follow to steal the Mercedes. If I am right, it would give me an excuse to return to the Tribal Police and pretend to search for the stolen car while looking for signs of Abu.

I passed by several Kewa Café billboards promoting their venison dinner special. It had been a while since I had venison so I pulled into the next Kewa Café on the way to the motel.

The next morning, my suspicions were confirmed as I came out of the motel room – the Mercedes was nowhere to be found. They had taken the bait. I reported the car stolen and filled out a police report. The police informed me they would be working with the rental company, so I could go on my way. Now I had the excuse I needed.

I rented another car. I must admit I was giddy driving to the reservation, knowing my plan had worked. I pulled up to the police station and took my time looking around before

I opened the weathered wooden door and entered. There he was. The same officer I spoke to the day before. Only now he was wearing his black long hair in a beaded ponytail with his name stitched on his shirt. *Machakw,* Hopi Indian, meaning *a horny toad.* I chuckled as he glanced up *as if to say, what the fuck do you want?*

"Hello, officer. I would like to report a stolen car," I said.

"You would?" Officer Machakw looked up at me with suspicion.

"Yes, it was taken by a couple of your braves," I said.

He pushed his chair back and said, "And how do you know that?"

"Have you seen a bright red Mercedes convertible driving around the reservation?" I asked.

The officer looked away and moved a few papers on his desk. "How did you get here?" Officer Machakw asked.

"I rented a car in hopes of finding mine. May I look around?" I boldly suggested.

He took a drink from his stained and cracked Casino-logoed cup. "Only members of the Indian Tribal Nation have the right to do that," Officer Machakw sneered and went back to the business of ignoring me. He pretended to fuss with his unimportant stack of papers.

I gained his attention when I spoke Comanche. "I'm a Comanche from the Lawton reservation in Oklahoma." Then I repeated it in English, knowing he didn't understand Comanche.

He was confused, seeing this blonde haired blue-eyed man hand him a Native American card. Officer Machakw became visibly pissed. He set his cup down so hard on the desk he spilled it over the useless papers. Then he slowly stood up, revealing his short box-shaped body in a very neat khaki shirt, pressed slacks, and red eel-skin boots. I didn't look like a Native American to anyone, let alone to another Native American.

"Could I check the area?" I politely asked.

Officer Machakw didn't say a word. He reached for his pinched-front straw cowboy hat sporting a beaded hatband displaying a silver cross. He grunted looking straight ahead, "You're one damn odd-looking Indian," Officer Machakw said. "I will drive."

I took that as a yes and followed him to his Wrangler police Jeep. Officer Machakw took his time adjusting the rearview mirror decorated with a string of beads holding a wooden cross. Most Native American Indians are Catholic and by the looks of the two rosary crosses, he was a devout one.

We drove through multiple dirt alleyways connecting the pueblo village. The area was sparse, with wild animals roaming, broken multi-colored shutters, and a web of clotheslines strung from one small adobe home to another. We drove by scattered homemade wooden truck beds built atop rusty old trucks, looking for the red Mercedes.

After an hour of frustration, I asked officer Machakw, "Where would you take it if it was you?"

He let out a deep sigh and looked down at the steering wheel, then forced the shifter into four-wheel drive. We headed up a kidney-crushing narrow mountain road. Not a word was spoken as we bumped along for miles before he stopped. "There." Officer Machakw pointed to another rock path split by two steep boulders wide enough for a car to drive through. He turned to me and said with his head tilted towards the steering wheel, "Whatever happens there is between you and them. Understand?"

"I promise it will be ugly," I scowled. Before I got out I notice an empty gallon size Ziploc® on the floor. I picked it up and asked, "Can I take this? "

Officer Machakw gave me a strange look and nodded yes and drove off mumbling, leaving me to mete out justice as I saw fit.

I examined the area, with the old Indian woman's face still floating in my head. It was clear to me the young braves were an embarrassment to their tribe. They would continue to prey on the old Indian woman for money, or even kill her, just for the glory of getting high.

I crawled over the rocks in the hot sun, making my way closer to the cave opening, careful not to make a sound. Five feet from the cave entrance, I heard faint voices—it sounded like four to five men. Then a voice with a German and Middle Eastern accent spoke. *That could be Abu*. My heart picked up a beat with the possibility that I might be right.

I placed my African finger knife with a seven-inch blade so sharp you would cut through the hide of a tiger in my calf-high right boot. Now it was all about the element of surprise.

I crawled through the entrance of the cave and spied four of them, including the two young braves. They were laughing and bragging to the others about how they stole the Mercedes from a white man at a motel. One was standing in the shadows. From this distance, he looked like Abu. He screamed in English an Arabic inflection at the two braves, "You stupid fools."

It could be Abu. I knew what I had to do. I took out my rosary and said a prayer. Then I stood up and walked into the cave, knowing Abu would recognize me. "So *this* is where you took my car, you bastards," I shouted.

The two young braves jumped up and froze. Then they ran at me. One pulled a small pistol and the other a large serrated hunting knife. The Mexican and Abu turned and ran away from the cave. I let out a shrieking Comanche war cry, causing the brave with the pistol to fire wildly, missing me as I cut his throat. The other brave sliced my hand with his serrated knife as I turned, lifting my elbow into his nose. I heard it crunch into his head as he dropped to my feet.

I ripped my shirt and wrapped my bloody hand and chased after the Mexican who was trying to climb the rocky hillside. He lost his footing and I pulled his head by his ears to my knee, knocking him out. The force of the blow cut his face open, covering it with blood. I rewrapped my hand as I chased after Abu. He had a head start and was quicker than I expected.

We ran over bush and sand as my right leg began to send sharp pains into my thigh, stopping me in my tracks. I quickly rubbed it and forced myself into a run again, fighting the pain by picturing, *Kele and myself running down a small deer on the reservation* as I struggled to keep my long strides.

I saw Abu had tripped and fallen to the hard desert ground. He looked to be out of breath from the high altitude. I picked up my pace. As he stood up, I was on him and seized a handful of his hair, pulling us both to the ground. "Now I finally have you," I said trying to capture more air to breathe.

He raised his hands pleading in broken English. "No. Please no," he repeated between taking in more air.

I turned his head, as I put my knife to his throat, to see his face. I shrieked, "You fuck." It wasn't Abu. It was Axel DeKlote. I screamed out in frustration, "Where is Abu?"

Axel recognized my face and said, "You should be dead."

I went out of my mind, pulling up his head by his hair and shouting in his face, "You can't kill me. Where is Abu?" He gazed stunned. I screamed louder, "Where is Abu?" He knew it was over and shut his eyes, refusing to say another word.

I pushed my knife along his forehead and began to cut into his flesh. Blood began to flow over his face, neck, and chest. He opened his eyes with renewed energy and spit into my face. I yanked him back toward me, holding his hair with my left hand, looking into his frightened eyes. Then he surprised me by kicking me in the nuts. He rolled on top of me and pounded his fists into my head, blood dropping on me from the cut in his forehead as he fought for my knife.

Axel wailed, "Fucking American. I will kill you." Twisting my arm behind me, he tried to take my knife. I let it go and reached behind my head, grasping a handful of Axel's hair, pulling him to my side. I started to roll on top of him, but my leg was numb. I forced myself up. Axel managed to find the knife on the ground and lunged toward my chest. He caught the skin, making a bloody slice along my chest. I kicked up and struck him in the temple, dazing him.

I took the knife after it fell from his hand and rolled over him again, speaking Arabic. "This is for Thomas." I placed my knife on his forehead as he lay motionless and started cutting. Before I peeled off his scalp, I shouted in his ear, "This is for Beirut." Then I violently yanked the scalp. It sounded like Velcro as I peeled it away from the crown of his head. He screamed so loud it echoed through the rocky hillside. I held up the patch of hair for him to see with the blood dripping on his face and said, "This is Comanche Justice."

I stomped on his knee until I heard it break. I managed to crawl to a rock and pulled myself up. I watched him try to get up, cursing me in

Arabic as his head started to bubble from the scorching heat and his face covered in blood. I rubbed my numb leg and took out the Ziploc® bag and placed the bloody scalp in it. I struggled, walking away, smelling the blood burning from his head. I knew it wouldn't be long before the wolves would smell the blood too, and come to feed on him, leaving what was left for the wild dogs and coyotes to fight over.

When I pulled up to the police station, officer Machakw was standing outside. He saw my face, hands, and chest splattered with blood. His face was drawn with fear. I handed officer Machakw the bloody Ziploc® bag with the scalp inside. "There's only one alive—a Mexican that will either die up there or find his way off the reservation," I said.

He held the bloody bag away from him flinching and frowned in disgust dropping it to the ground, giving me a ghost-like glare. "Are you fucking crazy?" he asked.

"You never saw a scalp before?" I asked. Then I saw the old Indian woman coming out of the market and I gave her a nod with my blood-splattered face, and drove off, listening to "The Bitch is Back." I left officer Machakw with a memento inside the Ziploc® bag to remember me by. *Unfortunately, my mind was possessed with finding Abu.*

"Excuse me." Senator Rouch from Idaho was colorless as he made a quick exit to the closest restroom. We all sat silently listening to the sounds of hacking, a toilet flush and water running. Then he returned and Jon quickly replaced his pitcher of water with fresh one. "Sorry," said Senator Rouch. He poured the much-needed glass of water saying, "Mr. Toscano, please go on."

CHAPTER 13

March 15, 1975,
Dallas, Texas

The master of ceremony announced, "Wearing the chic strapless with a plunging neckline is the Fashion Magazine's Aponi. This chiffon dress is by Native American designer Angeni with a one of a kind silver necklace and jewelry designed by Comanche Chief Peta."

I had made it back in time to clean up and photograph the fashion show. I was able to watch Aponi seducing the fashionable audience into a standing applause. It was exhilarating to see her six-foot walking canvas of beautiful red skin provide the fashion world with such an exotic image. The likes they have never seen before. Strutting down the stage, confidently showing her long bare legs and long black hair wearing a nighty for all to admire. Her black eyes proudly stared right back at the crowd. Most certainly Aponi was the star of the evening.

Afterward, I found Aponi backstage. “You make me and the Comanche Nation proud,” I told her and gave her a kiss. When I did the other paparazzi blinded us with a flood of rapid flashes. Exposing us as an item.

Pushing past them into her dressing room, Aponi said, “Kachada, my agent booked me for a shoot in Manhattan for a cosmetic deal.”

“When?” I asked as I closed the door, blocking the last camera flash.

“They would like to meet in two days. Can you come with me?” she asked. She saw my hand bandaged asking, “Kachada, what happened?”

I ignored it and said, “And be seen with the most beautiful woman of the decade? I think you know the answer to that.”

After the champagne and interviews, Aponi and I broke away and went directly to our hotel. I undid my bowtie and removed a few studs from my shirt as we walked into the Aldophus. The concierge came up and handed me a note. I put it in my pants pocket and walked to the elevators. "Aren't you going to read it?" Aponi asked.

"It can wait," I said.

"Kachada, read it," Aponi ordered. As we stepped onto the elevator I reluctantly opened it.

> Kachada, Meet me at PEUR DE RIEN in two days. Hayri.

"Well?" Aponi asked.

Not wanting to give her the bad news, I kept quiet. She grabbed my note and read it. "Who is this Hayri? Why Paris?" Aponi asked.

"Looks like you have to travel to New York without me," I said with remorse.

The elevator doors opened and she said, "Ah. You shouldn't have opened it." I stood by the elevator as Aponi stomped to the hotel suite, opening the door. She turned saying,

"Well?" Then I walked in. That night we exhausted ourselves making up, and the next day I caught a plane to Paris never explaining the wounded hand and cut along my chest.

On my walk to the magazine offices, an old BMW pulled up beside me. I leaned over and Hayri was at the wheel. "I didn't think you could drive," I said.

"I can't, but I needed to keep this meeting between us confidential," he said, Like a first-time driver holding the steering wheel so tight his knuckles were white.

"So you need me to drive?" I asked with a smile, hoping he would say yes. No luck.

Hayri said looking at my wrapped hand, "Kachada, doesn't look like you can drive with that hand, get in." He drove like a ninety-year-old woman, unable to grasp the perception of distance. Made for a whiplashing ride.

We finally ended the adventure on a lonely cobblestone street not far from *Notre Dame*. "Hayri, I feel like I was driving in a scene out of *Goldfinger*. What is it?" I asked.

"Kachada, this is the time to become invisible," Hayri said, still holding the steering wheel.

Stunned first by his driving and now by his comment, I asked, "Why fly me to Paris to tell me this?"

"I feel safer meeting in Paris. The word among the dark underworld is, you are on their list." He handed me a sealed manila envelope. I began to open it but he ordered, "Later when you are alone."

"What is it with you and this mysterious open later routine?"

He insisted, "Kachada, please. You will see."

The idea didn't appeal to me, but Hayri had always been someone I trusted. I placed the envelope inside my thin, waist-length black leather jacket and gladly got out of Hayri's car. I leaned into the open window and said, "I killed Axel. But Abu is still alive."

Hayri nodded, grasping the steering wheel and said, “That explains the hand and I know. We will talk.” He started to drive off when I yelled. “Try not to kill anyone driving.” Haryi was wiggling his way through the narrow street.

After he was out of sight I thought, *“How did he know? But then he did tell me he knows everything. Never quite sure how that's possible.”*

I flew directly to New York City and was walking into the Müller Agency in Manhattan to surprise Aponi when her agent Zoe ran up to me. “Kachada. What a surprise.” He gave me the typical fashion world kiss on both cheeks.

“I want to surprise Aponi. Can you tell me what studio she's in?” I asked.

He put his hand on my chest and said, “Kachada we arranged for a private jet to fly Aponi to Lawton. She got the news about Chief Peta.”

"What news?" I shouted.

"He's ill. That's all I know," Zoe said stepping back.

"I need to get a flight to Lawton," I said. *With my mind focused on Chief Peta.*

Zoe said, "Dear, don't worry, we will have a ticket waiting for you at the counter in LaGuardia."

I gave him a hug and said, "You're the best." I ran to the elevator as I heard Zoe say, "So I've been told."

Sitting next to the Chief holding my rosary, I prayed for his spirit. Aponi, Mom, and I took turns sitting by him for three days, praying he would open his eyes so we could tell him how much we loved him. But his eyes never opened.

The legacy of a great Comanche Chief, warrior, a renowned artist, and grandfather would forever live in our hearts. The night-long celebration brought the Comanche

Nation and art gallery representatives from around the world to celebrate his loss. It was a sad, but proud day for the Comanche Nation.

Aponi sat next to me wearing her native buckskin and boots at Grandpa's table. Mom sensed our connection. "Kacahda. You know it is an honor to marry after celebrating the Chief's spirit joining his ancestors?" she said.

Aponi gave me a smile. I knew what I needed to do. But I came with baggage. Mom left us alone. I held Aponi and said, "Aponi, I love you but . . ."

Aponi quickly interrupted me. "Kachada. Your mother knows. Chief Peta knew. You and I know we are meant to be together."

I started to say, "But there is . . ."

Again she interrupted me. "I know about your diagnosis. My heart is yours, and yours is mine. Nothing can change that. Ever since that moment we kissed and made love at Chief Peta's."

But she doesn't know everything about Hayri and me. "Aponi, there is more," I said.

I had to be careful what I said. But if I were to marry Aponi she needed to know. I began to explain my connection to Hayri, and how we met. How I had joined Hayri's team to find the terrorists who were looking for me.

She sat quietly, listening. Afterward, she got up and closed the door. Then started taking off her clothes. She walked to me and pressed herself into me and whispered. "Let's not waste any minutes we have together." She pushed me onto the floor and we melted together.

The tribesmen and women mourning Chief Peta chanted to the spirits. The Chief was wrapped in his ceremonial blanket and headdress, his face painted as a warrior going into battle. He faced up towards the night sky. Kele gave Mom the honor of chanting to the spirits. "Kachada. Aponi. Join me," Mom asked. Aponi and I stood next to her chanting.

After the ceremony, the Chief's body was taken from the tree branch scaffolding and placed in the Comanche burial grounds next to his ancestors. That night the celebration continued by burning Chief Peta's headdress, blanket, spear and warrior necklace. We gazed at the ashes floating up into the night sky against the bright stars. The image of the smoke from the burning flames circling up like wisps mesmerized me. It made me proud to be Comanche. The celebration went into the next morning with tribal chants and eating customary Comanche delicacies of deer cooked over the fire with prairie turnips, corn, and potatoes flavored with wild herbs cooked in a stew pot. It was a menu the visiting art dignitaries forced themselves to adjust to.

The next morning, the crowd dispersed. Aponi and I said goodbye to the art crowd and her fashion friends, returning the reservation back to its unassuming status. Mom came up to me and asked, "Kachada. Do you have something to tell me?"

"I love Aponi. But I am afraid of what my future is," I confessed.

"The future is now. You've been counting the minutes alone for too long. Now you need someone to count them with you together." She then said, "It's not just about you."

Standing in fringed buckskin tunic and leggings with breechcloths made of buffalo hide, the tribal men braided my hair into two long braids. Kele placed the Chief's war bonnet on me. It was decorated with eagle feathers and ermine tails trailing behind.

The drums began to pound melodically with the setting sun. Kele puts his hands on my shoulders. "My brother, I pray you are blessed with healthy young warriors." He walked me to the ceremony where the fire was blazing high into the sky and Mom was waiting. The tribal women chanted to the beats of the drum. Kele placed me two steps behind Mom. It was the first time I had seen

Mom so excited. She was wearing her ceremonial Comanche buckskin, with her hair in a single braid with a hawk feather and decorated leggings.

From Aponi's teepee, a line of women formed a circle around her, hiding her face until she arrived. They encircled me, chanting, and then danced off in a single line, leaving Aponi and me standing side by side. We were careful not to touch. I stole a glance and my heart beat so fast I started to sweat. Aponi stood tall and stoic, looking straight ahead, daring not to look at me. The image of her in the knee-length buckskin dress with fringe and decorated leggings reminded me how I lucky I was. Her hair was in two thick braids decorated with beads. The women decorated her dress with colorful painted signs and symbols, honoring Chief Peta and our Comanche ancestors. They presented her with the traditional beaded hair pipe breastplate. Her six-foot frame was a stunning image of beauty.

Kele proceeded with the ceremony, chanting the tribal rituals. The ceremony seemed as though it went on forever. I just wanted it to end so I could take her and ride off into the sunset like the happy ending of a John Ford western. But I knew there was no happy ending waiting for me.

Kele ended the ritual and said, "Aponi and Kachada, you are now one." For the first time during the ceremony, we turned and looked into each other's eyes. I pushed her long braids aside and kissed her. The drums and chants pounded louder, beginning the celebration of happiness. Neither of us was allowed to speak.

The tribal women escorted us to a teepee they had decorated for us. Inside was the traditional fire with buffalo blankets spread out. Once inside, the women undressed us and rubbed us down with oil made from local flowers. They lay Aponi down and signaled for me to join her. It was the Comanche tradition we consummate the marriage as the women watched. They chanted and shook their rattles until we bonded as one. I held Aponi and said, "I promise to battle for every new minute of my life."

Aponi held me and said; "Now we can fight together."

Aponi and I agreed to try and keep our marriage as low profile as possible her image had catapulted her to tabloid fame. Her face and body were on all the magazine covers. During interviews, she never mentioned my name. I stayed away from the awards and the eyes of the paparazzi. Images had surfaced from the Dallas fashion show where the paparazzi had captured us together, making it more difficult.

"Hold on," Senator Wyatt piped up. "I just realized you are talking about the famous model from the eighties. Aponi. Right?" she asked.

"Yes," I said simply.

"She was your wife?" Senator Wyatt said in amazement.

"I know. Not what you would have expected," I said.

Senator Cornwall said, "If I recall, she was mysteriously killed."

I held my tongue. "She was," I said.

"Mr. Toscano, "I am so sorry," Senator Wyatt said.

"Me too," I said and continued with my story.

I spent time on the reservation and in Manhattan with Aponi but kept away from the public eye. During one trip to Manhattan, I treated myself to MoMA. Standing in front of Matisse's *The Open Window,* I felt a tap on my shoulder. Not knowing what to expect, I turned to see Aponi standing there all smiles.

"Aponi. Why are you here?" I asked.

"You think I have no appreciation for art?" she snickered.

"No. No. I…"

She puts her finger on my mouth, "Shh. Just listen." She wrapped her arms around me to whisper into my ear.

"What?" I said. The news she had just given me was so shocking I didn't know what to think.

She frowned, not expecting my response. "Kachada, I thought you would be happy."

I could see the hurt in her eyes. I pulled her into me and said, "I love you so much."

She pushed me away and said, "Don't be so selfish." Then walked away.

"Aponi." I ran after her and found her sitting on a chair crying in a small hallway hidden from the public. I was broken seeing her so upset. "I love you. I want what you want."

"I want us to want," Aponi responded, not looking at me.

"I can't promise you I will be here to help raise a child," I said hanging my head.

"I know," Aponi said. "I want this child to be our legacy. He will be with me when you are not." Aponi stood up to hold me.

I held her tight, thinking, *I never thought about her. I was so selfish I only thought about me.*

Aponi whispered in my ear, "I have a name."

I laughed, saying. "I can't wait to hear it."

She whispered, "Knoton. It means . . ."

"I know," I said, "Wind." I kissed her face, damp from crying, and stared at Matisse's *Gold Fish.* The family of three swimming fish made me chuckle. From that point on we did everything in public, hiding nothing.

With Hayri's encouragement, I decided to take a creative director position in Atlanta. The job allowed me to travel internationally—but most importantly, Atlanta was only a two-hour flight from the reservation. *Abu was still lurking in the back of my mind.* I was determined to find him so I could be with my family and never worry about him harming them.

We had moved to a beautiful development just north of Atlanta, along the Chattahoochee River, called Neely Farms. It was made up of two-story brick and stucco homes surrounded by lush green lawns, wide sidewalks, nestled among tall southern pines. We claimed a house on a cul de sac. It was our slice of the American dream and the perfect neighborhood to start a family.

I worked long hours developing a new campaign for our Delta Airlines client. We sold them a series of thirty-second TV spots promoting their international business travel. The campaign took us to Dallas, Kennedy, O'Hare, LAX, San Francisco, Heathrow, with the last stop at Charles de Gaulle Airport. The spots rallied around the tagline, "To Europe and back on time."

While on production in Manhattan, I received a call to fly home. Aponi had gone into labor early. I arrived in Atlanta just in time for the birth of our son. Both nervous and anxious, I stood in the delivery room holding Aponi's hand. I listened to the familiar noise of the doctor and nurses going about their business of bringing a new life into our world. Aponi's beautiful black eyes fixed on mine never crying out as she gave birth.

The nurse called out his vitals. "Weight: seven pounds eight ounces. Twenty-three inches tall—a big boy!"

Aponi took him into her arms and cooed into his little pink ears. She whispered, "Knoton is Comanche for *wind*. May the spirit of your soul soar forever."

The sight of her kissing and cooing in his ears returned me to my first breath. *My mother whispering, "Kachada: Remember, birth is a death sentence. So make every minute count."*

I know in my heart that my son heard Aponi and will remember everything just as I did. Aponi's words, her smile, and her tears of joy would comfort him when he recalls this moment. They won't haunt him like mine did. After giving Aponi another kiss, I left the room, giving her a much-needed rest.

In the hallway, I looked out the fourth-floor window overlooking North Atlanta. I sank into a comfortable leather chair. My mind was exhausted with so many emotions. "Mr. Toscano? Mr. Toscano." A young nurse tapped me. "Mr. Toscano."

I jumped up. "Yes, what? Is anything wrong?" I asked.

"Oh, no, I'm sorry if I scared you," The nurse apologized.

"What?" I demanded while climbing out of my trance.

The nurse said, "Your wife asked if you would join her."

Relieved, I said, "Yes, yes, of course, I will." I was still trying to clear my eyes as she brought out Aponi in a wheelchair. We held hands as Aponi shed joyful tears. My eyes swelled, thanking her for making me what I never thought I would ever live to become. *A father.*

CHAPTER 14

October 22, 1975, Norcross, Georgia

"Welcome aboard," said the stewardess. I showed her my ticket. "Mr. Toscano, seat 4 B. Enjoy the flight to New York City."

"Thank you." I relaxed in the large leather first-class seat and put my head back, thinking about Aponi and our son Knoton.

"Mr. Toscano, can I get you a drink after we take off?" the sweet young face with blonde hair and beautiful hazel eyes, asked me.

"A Bloody Mary, please." Then I asked, "What is your name?"

"Jennifer. I'll have your drink as soon as everyone settles after takeoff." She went about her business of taking care of the next passenger. I was flying back to New York City to start production on the Delta campaign. During the two-hour flight, I relaxed closing my eyes, reliving the birth of my son.

"Mr. Toscano," a voice said.

I opened my eyes and glanced up at the sweet face of Jennifer. "You remembered," I said.

She gave me her sweet smile. "Sorry, it took me longer than usual. Your Bloody Mary."

"Thank you."

She tapped me on the shoulder. "If you need any assistance hit this call button." She returned to her other passengers.

I opened a paperback I found placed in the seat's back pocket, *Poirot's Last Case* by Agatha Christie, and began reading:

> Elizabeth Cole tells Hastings she is a sister of Margaret Litchfield, who confessed . . .

The pilot broke in, "We should be landing in LaGuardia in less than thirty minutes.

The stewardess will come around and pick up any trash and make sure your seats and tray tables are in the upright position for landing. We at Delta Airlines hope you had an enjoyable flight to the city that never sleeps. And we hope to be your airline of choice on your next trip."

I returned the paperback to the seat pocket, taking the last sip of my Bloody Mary. I got up to put my garbage in the kitchen area when a shrill scream erupted from the back of the plane. Standing by my seat, I noticed my smiling stewardess was now wearing a face of terror. A short, slender man had a sharp object pressed to her throat. The other passengers were screaming in their seats. Just then, a brave middle-aged man started to move towards the stewardess. The terrorist made a gesture, threatening to slit her throat, giving the brave man no other choice but to retreat to his seat.

Jennifer's face was pink from crying. My blood vessels were popping as I watched the poor girl's face. I counted two men: one was holding a pistol, the other the stewardess. They started to back up towards first class. I recognized one man's Russian-made Makarov and the other man holding a sharp piece of metal next to her throat. The men growled back and forth in German. I couldn't make out what they are saying as they made their way towards the cockpit. It was obvious they intended to hijack the plane. I knew there was no way they would get what they wanted. Pilots were given strict instructions never to open the cockpit door under any circumstances. This was not going to end well.

The two terrorists slowly backed towards the front of the plane. I sat, waiting, as the one with the pistol came up behind the other, closing in on my seat. I remained still. The terrorist holding the stewardess pulled her in front of him, focused on the passengers as he walked backward, keeping them at bay. The passengers were afraid the terrorist would kill the young girl if they made any advances. My eyes caught Jennifer's as she passed by my seat, so different from when she handed me my Bloody Mary. After both passed by me, I thought *what if Aponi and Konton were on this plane. What would I want someone to do?*

I flexed my fingers, thinking about what I needed to do. *First, I needed to attack the terrorist with the knife, and then take out the one holding the Makarov. I only had six seconds or less before they reacted. If I failed Jennifer could be killed and the entire plane would turn into a horrific scene.*

I tightened my index fingers as my only weapon. I had to wait for the right moment. I knew my move had to be powerful, accurate and quick.

I kept my eyes glued to the one holding Jennifer and started counting in my head. *One Mississippi, two Mississippi, three Miss*—suddenly the plane hit an air pocket, causing both men to go off balance. I took advantage of the fortunate moment and lunged into action. I thrust myself into the one with the knife and pushed Jennifer aside, ripping his throat out while simultaneously shoving my left hand into the other man's chin as he fired his pistol hitting the food cart. I clenched my hand on his jawbone and pulled down. Blood splattered onto the passengers sitting nearby. The sound of bones snapping and screams ended within four seconds.

The stewardess, shaken, fell to the floor and crawled up the aisle. Others jumped out of their seats to help her into a seat before she passed out from shock. A doctor on the plane ran over to help. The two terrorists lay collapsed in the aisle, barely alive, their eyes bouncing. Another passenger came running towards the terrorists to help them. I scowled, ordering her, "Go back to your seat." She glanced down at their bloody faces, then at my blood-splattered shirt, face and arms, and retreated to her seat.

I kneeled between the two, speaking German. "Who are you?" I asked. Their eyes were twitching. "Why this plane?" I asked. The one with the makeshift knife *tried to say something as if to save* his soul and gurgled, "in the name of Allah" and then said, "Praise Abu." Then hell took him.

I went to the lavatory and washed the blood from my hands and face. The commotion was over and we were beginning our landing. So I quickly sat back in my seat and buckled up. The two Abu disciples were lying dead in their own pools of blood. It was a surreal scene. *If only I could have killed Abu in Beirut when I had the chance. I promised myself then I had to find Abu and kill him before more innocent people like Jennifer suffered from his inhumane attacks.*

While waiting at a gate roped off next to a restaurant to be questioned by the FBI and the NYPD, Jennifer came from behind the closed restaurant door and saw me. She started weeping and ran to give me a warm hug. "I thought I was going to die," she said between gasps of whimpering breaths.

Thinking of *Aponi and Knoton,* "not today," I said holding her.

She pulled back and said, "Thanks to you, I'll be getting married next week." The thought of this sweet young girl almost dying before her wedding day pained me.

The moment was interrupted when a woman in a dark suit with an FBI badge around her neck walked up to me and asked, "Mr. Toscano?"

I waited for a moment. "Yes," I replied.

"You sure? You hesitated," she asked.

I glared for only a moment and said, "Sorry, it's been a strange day."

She nodded. "I should say so. I am FBI agent Howard." She held the ID hanging around her neck up. "Sorry to keep you waiting until last. Please follow me." She turned and started walking to the door. I gave the stewardess one last hug and followed Agent Howard into the makeshift interview room. There were three others waiting inside. A New York City officer stood behind two men sitting at the table in dark suits.

A tall man who looked to be thirty-something stood up and said, "Mr. Toscano? I am agent Zucco. Please sit down." Agent Zucco presented his handsome friendly smile, supported by his thick salt and pepper hair, and olive skin.

I sat down, observing their faces. The younger agent sitting to the left of the female agent introduced himself. "Mr. Toscano, I am Agent Pavlic." Then he pointed to the officer standing behind them with the dark beard and said, "This is Officer McGarrity." The officer gave me a nod. Agent Pavlic sat down, looking at his college-lined notepad and said, "You have already met Agent Howard."

"Yes, we met," I said.

"We would like you to give us your account of the incident on Delta Flight 121. Mr. Toscano, it is my duty to inform you that you are being recorded during our conversation. Do you understand what I just said, Mr. Toscano?" Agent Pavlic asked.

"Yes, of course. Not a problem," I replied.

The questions started. "Mr. Toscano, why did you choose this flight?" asked agent Pavlic.

I answered, "It was the last flight from Atlanta to Manhattan."

"Why Manhattan? Mr. Toscano?" Agent Pavlic asked.

Annoyed I said, "To prepare for a shoot. Ah, sorry. That's film lingo. I am filming a series of commercials for Delta Airlines."

"Oh. So you work for Delta?" Asked agent Howard.

"Yes and no. I work for RMDS. We are the ad agency for Delta," I said.

"What would you like us to call you? Mr. Toscano? Kachada?" asked Agent Howard

"Mr. Toscano would be fine, thank you."

Officer McGarrity blurted out, "We understand that you saved the passengers by attacking and killing both terrorists." The agents were annoyed that he had interrupted their questioning.

"Yes, sir," I said.

Agent Zucco gathered himself and said, "Quite a display of bravery and talent."

Agent Howard asked, "How did you do that Mr. Toscano?"

I bit my lip knowing my answer would be a problem. "My hand's ma'am," I said with hesitation.

"Sorry, would you repeat that, Mr. Toscano? You may call me Agent Howard," she insisted.

"Of course. Agent Howard. My hands, Agent Howard," I said.

Agent Pavlic looking with squinted eyes, and asked, "And where did you learn those skills?"

"Martial arts has been a passion of mine since my teenage years, Agent Pavlic," I said.

"What martial arts did you use on the flight?" asked Agent Pavlic.

At this point, I knew my name would be on the FBI watch list. I hesitated.

"Mr. Toscano do I need to repeat the question?" Agent Pavlic asked.

I hesitated again and finally said, "A combination of taekwondo and krav maga."

Agent Pavlic was surprised, as were the others in the room. "Really? Quite a combination for anyone, let alone a civilian, Mr. Toscano," Agent Zucco said.

I asked, "Am I in trouble here?"

Agent Zucco spoke up, "Should you be?"

"No," I responded.

Looking down at her notepad, then up towards me, Agent Howard said, "Mr. Toscano you saved the lives of a hundred and fifty people on Flight 121 tonight." She sighed, "To those people, you are a hero." Agent Howard took another pause before continuing, "To us, we saw one terrorist with his throat ripped out, and another with his jaw dangling from his face. In all my years I have never seen anyone do what you did by using only your bare hands."

Agent Pavlic then said, "We estimate, from our interviews with the passengers, it took you six seconds. So, Mr. Toscano, you can understand why you have captured our attention."

Since I'd already captured their attention, I decided to set the record straight. "Four seconds, agent," I said.

"What did you say?" asked Agent Howard.

"It took me four seconds," I said.

Agent Pavlic leaning back in his chair asked, "Four seconds?"

I lost it and just blurted out what was on my mind, "I fucking did what needed to be done." I became animated. "They stood right next to my seat. My wife just gave birth to my son and I promised myself I was not going to fucking die today," I shouted.

They sat quietly until Agent Zucco broke the silence. "You, Mr. Toscano, are a very brave and dangerous man."

I retaliated, "Agent Howard said I saved one hundred fifty passengers."

"You did, Mr. Toscano," Agent Pavlic said with a smile.

"Who were the terrorists?" I asked.

"Our agents are looking into their background," Agent Howard said.

I fixed my ice-blue eyes on Agent Pavlic. "What else do you need?" I asked.

Agent Pavlic stared, "Nothing, Mr. Toscano. You are free to go, for now. We appreciate your cooperation, and for Agent Howard, Zucco, Officer McGarrity, and on behalf of the FBI and the New York Police Department, we thank you for taking it upon yourself to save all those innocent passengers. You will need to leave us your contact information so we can reach you."

I knew they had already gathered it before they brought me in. "What did you mean for now and why would you need me?" I asked.

"It may be necessary for you to give your account of what happened. It would be private, behind closed doors. No media. No publicity. Only the FBI and possibly the CIA," said agent Howard.

"Don't take this the wrong way, but I hope I never meet any of you again," I said.

"None taken Mr. Toscano. We wish you a good day and safe travels," said agent Zucco. I got up and left for the taxi stand. Now that I had the attention of the FBI and maybe the CIA, I needed to warn Hayri.

CHAPTER 15

October 22, 1975,
Midtown Manhattan

After being dropped off at the Paramount Hotel in Midtown Manhattan, I checked in, fell on the bed, and called Aponi to make sure she and Knoton were doing okay. I choose not to mention the incident on the plane. There were no reports on the local and national news about the hijacking attempt. The FBI was keeping a tight lid on it for now.

Surrounded by the rush of energy during my cold morning walk down Broadway, I passed

Macy's. This brought back memories of me watching the Thanksgiving Day Parade with Grandpa Giovanni. We would eat steamed mussels and linguine instead of turkey and stuffing.

At Broadway and 22nd Street, I met with the director, Schein. He was impressed I spoke Polish making our discussion about the shot list much easier. During the meeting, he introduced me to Zane, the director of photography from Vienna. Zane was a handsome thirty-something blond-haired, blue-eyed Austrian with an infatuating smile. We quickly hit it off and discovered we both loved art.

We wrapped up our shot list in New York and moved on to Chicago, then Dallas, then Los Angeles. San Francisco was our final stop in the states. We spent the first day climbing to the top of the Golden Gate Bridge to film the impressive skyline with a hand-held camera. I was three weeks into the project, and getting daily updates from Aponi. It gave me peace of mind knowing they were enjoying their new home in Atlanta.

Our first location in Europe was Paris. The *City of Love* had become my home away from home. I was looking forward to having dinner with my good friend, Hayri. There was much to talk about since the LaGuardia incident.

I settled in at the Hotel du Petit Moulin, set in a stylish area of Paris because it was only a short walk to the Musee National Picasso and the Eiffel Tower.

I was surprised by a knock at my door, the concierge handed me a note with my name written on it. "Monsieur," the concierge said.

"Je vous remercie." I said and handed him a tip.

I recognized Hayri's handwriting:

> My friend,
>
> After you arrive, I will be at La Petite Table. As always, I am looking forward to seeing you. Hayri.

I freshened up and walked to La Petit with a bounce in my step, pleased to be in Paris. Hayri was waiting, waving from his table. He wore a suave-looking expensive Parisian suit with his thick black hair wet and combed back. We did the traditional French greeting.

Hayri was quick to say, "Aponi and Knoton look good on you, Kachada."

"Yes. I feel good, Hayri," I said.

Hayri smiled. "It is good to see you happy. I would like to meet them someday."

I suggested, "Ma maison est ta maison." *My house is your house.*

I could see Hayri was touched. "Kachada, I would like that." Then he turned our conversation to business. "I know what happened on Flight 121."

I conceded a smile of confession. "I'm not surprised. How? No information has been released."

"Not publicly. But the underground media travels fast my friend. Which means Hezbollah and Al Qaeda have a pipeline to the same rumors," Hayri said with concern.

"My name has not been released," I said.

Hayri informed me the terrorists were a faction from Belgium. He explained, "If I can identify you as the passenger on the flight, so can they."

"The terrorists are dead," I said.

Hayri pointed out, "There are ways of getting the passenger list. It would only be a matter of time to track the names and identify you."

"Hayri. Remember, I was left for shark food," I said.

Hayri let out a bellowing laugh. "It wouldn't be the first time in our business a dead man returned from the dead."

I wasn't so jovial about his comment and said, "So you think I'm fucked?"

"No, Kachada. Listen, I am making you aware of the danger. This life may not be for you now. You have a family to protect," Hayri said.

"I appreciate your concern, but during that incident, I kept thinking, what if Aponi and Knoton were on this flight? I would hope someone would be there to save them. Besides Aponi understands."

"Kachada, Aponi *knows*?" Hayri asked.

"Yes, I had to tell her before we got married."

Hayri looked worried, saying, "An understanding woman, but also dangerous *for you*."

I reminded Hayri, "Aponi is Comanche."

"Kachada, please excuse me, but don't you think you should spend the time you have left with them?" Hayri said.

"Hayri, I have lived 962,160 minutes longer than anyone expected me to." I took a long breath and said, "I must find Abu."

Hayri understood me and made the perfect transition. "The enemy you speak of, Kachada, Farid Khan, is one of Abu's officers and believed to be the architect of the November 17th attack on the Intercontinental Hotel in Amman, Jordan. Two Jordanian soldiers and two civilians were killed."

"Hayri." I leaned in to speak in a lower tone, "Abu."

Hayri was befuddled. "What about Abu?"

"I'm sure one of the terrorists on the plane *gurgled* the name Abu," I whispered.

Hayri enlightened. "The hijacking is typical of Abu. All the more reason we need to find Farid. If you're right, he may be the one who coordinated the attack."

"Farid. You never mentioned his name before," I said.

Hayri ran his fingers through his hair, "Remember the day we first met in Zurich?" he asked.

I chuckled. "I felt sorry for you. You looked . . . so disheveled," I said.

Hayri gave me a quizzical look and said, "Farid is Abu's cousin and his right-hand man. His father, Mohammad Khan, and Hanni Naif planned the attack in Istanbul responsible for killing my entire family."

A pause came over us both. I knew how killing Farid would help close that chapter for Hayri. "Are you sure?" I asked.

"Yes," Hayri said. "I have been tracking his family and their involvement with Abu's organization. The terrorist that muttered Abu's name makes sense. I had heard a rumor Farid was planning an attack.

"Do you think the Delta flight was the attack?" I asked.

"I will know more by tomorrow. Can we meet then?" Hayri asked.

"I should be back to my hotel by 6:00 p.m. would that work?" I asked.

"Yes." Hayri got up and said, "I will leave you to your espresso."

Watching him walk away I replayed his words. *"Responsible for killing my entire family."*

Just as I returned to my hotel from my meetings there was a knock at my door. "Hayri, come in," I said.

"How was your day?" Hayri asked.

"It's Paris. Every day is more beautiful than the next," I said.

"Yes, Paris," Hayri sighed. "I have located Farid. He has been seen in Roses, a city in the province of Girona, Spain."

"Never heard of it," I admitted.

"It is a beautiful village along the north-east coast, off the Balearic Sea. I have an address where Farid was seen—a small villa close to the promenade, at 44 Avenue de la Riera Ginjolers, off Carrer d'en Mairo. He is with a lady friend he brought from Barcelona."

"What do you mean?" I asked.

Hayri said, "My resources inform me she is a high-priced escort who knows nothing about Farid or what he does."

"An expensive traveling partner," I said.

"Indeed. I bought you a round-trip ticket on KLM. It leaves first thing Saturday," Hayri then said. "A beautiful place to kill what you call an ugly beast." Hayri continued, "I have you booked into the Prestige Mary Sol Hotel Elit on Placa de Catalunya."

"Huh, Beauty and the Ugly Beast," I said as an aside.

"Kachada." Haryi shook his head, taking an uncomfortable pause. "You have a way about you. Now, on a serious note, you need to be careful."

I gave him a shoulder shrug. "Sure."

Hayri grabbed me. "I'm serious. You have a family now."

Surprised by his reaction I assured him, "I will be careful."

Hayri demanded, "Promise."

"Hayri, I promise," I said.

Hayri added, '"A painful death would be appreciated." We hugged and Hayri said, "God bless you," and left.

I drove forty-some miles north from Girona-Costa Brava Airport through the beautiful scenery of northern Spain. After I checked into the hotel in Roses, I walked along the white sandy beaches looking toward the Mediterranean, thinking *about how Abu got away in Beirut.*

Weaving my way through the quaint streets to the villas lining the street, one next to the other, I noticed a Vespa parked alongside one. It was the address Hayri gave me. This was the off-season for vacationers and the streets were quiet, making my meeting with Farid far less risky.

The one-floor villa had a screen door as the front entrance. Access would not be a problem. It was obvious to me that Farid believed he was safe lodging in the quiet village of Roses.

A small bicycle rental shop across the street from the row of villas provided me with the perfect observation tool. I rented a bike, riding it around the small village, exploring the area while keeping an eye out for any unusual activity. After a few rides along the streets, I passed by Farid's villa just as a beautiful young girl emerged. She seated herself on the Vespa and rode off out of my eyesight. I was sure this was the escort Hayri told me about. But I needed to be sure Farid was inside. So I continued my bike tour.

It wasn't long before I heard the whining sound of the Vespa returning. I peddled back towards Farid's villa and saw the young woman carrying a long baguette. I knew someone else was inside—Farid. I decided to wait, praying the girl might leave to spare her from being killed. I couldn't leave anyone inside Farid's villa alive.

I returned to the hotel to prepare for my meeting with Farid. I had promised Hayri to make it painful. I put latex gloves on and carefully took a pen box from my travel bag. Inside, I had turned the pen into a vial filled with chironex fleckeri a potent venom from a rare species of jellyfish.

Before leaving for Rose I had gone to the Val d'Europe. It was there Elodie introduced me to a Marine Biologist friend named Acel Dubois. During our visit, he explained how the rare jellyfish excreted one of the most-wicked venoms in the world for self-defense.

When I promised Hayri I would make it a painful experience for Farid, I knew the jellyfish venom would be perfect. I paid Acel a handsome sum of money for the venom and his silence. I knew after watching him count the money I had nothing to worry about.

I carefully took the pen from the box and stuck it with a syringe drawing only 1mL. According to Acel, 1mL should be enough. But I didn't want to take any chances so I made it 1.5mL. According to Acel, the venom would cause Farid to become paralyzed, making his heart expand and explode, mimicking a painful heart attack.

If I was going to make the last flight to Paris before my Monday morning production meeting, I needed to be careful of my timing. I pulled my rosary from my pants pocket and said a prayer. A ritual of mine, praying for the souls my target had taken. May they rest in peace.

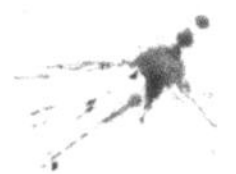

The late afternoon breeze made for a pleasant ride. I dropped off the bike at the rental shop and wasted no time walking to the villa. Once I arrived at the screen door, I didn't hesitate. I opened the door and went inside, catching the naked young woman coming out of the bathroom. I immediately punched her before she could turn to see me. She lay unconscious. In one seamless motion, I kicked open the bedroom door, where I expected to find Farid.

Fuck. I was frustrated to see he was not alone. Two young men were in bed with him. I had to keep to my plan.

Without hesitation, I took one by the hair and engulfed his head, snapping his neck. I then stuck the other's face with the back of my hand, followed by a strike to his throat. He gasped and began choking to death. I stuck him in the throat again to make his death less painful. I turned and saw that Farid had jumped to his feet, reaching for a TT-30 Russian pistol lying on the nightstand. I tossed his limp lover to the side and leaped over the bed as he fired a shot that grazes my arm.

Farid's naked body was excreting shit as he panicked and ran towards the front door, screaming in Arabic. I had to get to him before he made it out of the villa. I bolted after him and made a desperate leap to kick him in the back. I knocked him into the door, causing the TT-30 to slide across the floor. I dragged him away from the front door and kicked him between the legs, causing him to roll into the fetal position. I pulled the syringe from my cloth belt and forced his head to the side while he still held his testicles. I stuck his neck and squeezed the 1.5mL of the venom into his body while holding his nose with my hand. I noticed the blood flowing onto Farid from the gunshot wound in my arm. I stood up and clenched my hand around my arm. Farid jumped to his feet, causing me to flinch back, scaring the shit out of me. A reaction Acel forgot to mention.

Just as fast as he jumped up, he fell back to the floor. Still getting over the shock of his reaction, I leaned down to make sure the venom was taking effect. His eyes bounced left to right. Speaking French, I said, "Your heart will explode inside your chest, causing a painful death. This is for your sins and your father's sins for the 1955 killing of the Francisco Thorin family in Zurich." His eyes twitched.

His chest expanded and then there was a hard thump. He sat up and tried to scream but nothing came out. His eyes revolved rapidly for about four seconds before they became still. He collapsed to the floor with blood dripping from his nose and ears. Farid was dead. I turned my attention to the girl lying limp on the floor. Her teeth were spread out next to her head. The two extra bodies I hadn't planned for posed a problem. I left 70,000 Spanish Pesetas next to the unconscious girl on the floor for a dentist. She hadn't seen my face. So I saw no reason to kill the innocent girl.

What to do with the other two bodies? I scouted the area behind the villa, aware of my limited time. I found a dried-out well in the neighbor's backyard. I knocked several times on their back door before I forced it open. The only family I found living inside was mice.

I returned to Farid's villa and wrapped my arm in a pillowcase, then cleaned up the small splatters of blood on the floor leaving the villa spotless. After wrapping each of the two bodies in a sheet, I took them one at a time and dropped them down the neighbor's well. I returned to Farid and positioned him on the bed to make his death look as natural as possible. I stepped over the girl, making sure she was still unconscious and walked out the door. I knew the girl would be gone before the police would discover Farid's body. I also knew the police would not want the quiet reputation of their resort town to be a distraction to future vacationers.

On my flight to Paris, I kept using the restroom to clean my arm to keep it from bleeding and decided not to tell Hayri about leaving the escort alive. She was just at the wrong place at the wrong time. I convinced myself I had done the right thing.

On Monday morning I had my arm in a sling when I met with the production team. Zane asked about it and I just said it was a sprain. Then he told me the client asked us to pull London from our shot list. We finished up in Paris and I flew back to New York City.

My schedule allowed me ten working days to finish the spots and make our deadline. I spent two hours each day approving and giving advice and returned the next morning to repeat the same process. The routine gave me free time to enjoy my favorite pastime, a visit to the MoMA.

I kept the hotel room and flew home for the weekends. Aponi asked about my bandaged arm and I told her I fell off the camera car during a shot in Paris. Since the birth of Knoton, I was trying everything I could to extend my life. I became a mad scientist and used what Chief Peta taught me about the value of natural cures, mixing exotic roots and plants. I used different concoctions to give me more energy. The only pain relief I found was smoking marijuana. As time went on, I experimented with more potent weed. I was determined to live as long as possible and manage my pain so that I could watch my son Knoton grow up.

On a flight back to New York City after visiting my family, I held my rosary admiring my grandfather's craftsmanship. During the flight, I recalled my grandfather handing me the rosary and saying: *Kachada, this is to remind you your Comanche and Sicilian spirit are always with you.*

I was admiring the Henri de Toulouse-Lautrec sketches at the MoMA when my antennae went up. Two men in black had been following me from one part of the show to the other. I thought about what Hayri had said. *You have a family to protect.* But I tried not to become paranoid over it.

I left the art gallery and took the long way back to my hotel, making sure no one was following me. Once inside my hotel room, I turned on the lights and heard, "Kachada, so glad to see you." the voice said.

It was a voice I knew. Startled I saw Zane, the director of photography from my Delta project sitting in one of the soft chairs in my living area. "Why are you here? And how . . ."

Before I could finish, Zane cut me off. "I asked the front desk to let me in." I stood in the doorway, not saying a word. "I know who you are and what you've done," Zane said.

I asked, "What do you know?"

"I have known about you since the Delta hijacking attempt," Zane said.

I remained calm *thinking, my fears have come true.* Zane pulled out an ID card and placed it on the small table next to his chair. Cautiously, I walked over and picked it up with my sore arm. "I am supposed to believe this is real?" I said.

Zane smiled and said, "It's real. And you know it. And how is that arm of yours?"

I ignored the arm comment and asked, "Did you have me followed today?"

"I did," Zane replied. "Ever since the Delta flight."

I asked, "Which one are you working with? Agent Zucco? Agent Howard? Ah,

Agent Pavlic. He seemed like the leader of the group."

"If you must know, none of them. My orders came from a much higher-level. The Delta incident was just a coincidence. But it also confirmed to them you are one very dangerous man." He turned away and sat back into the chair with an arrogant smile. "And Kachada, that's why I am here."

I held the card staring at his headshot:

Zane Kendrick
Special Agent CIA 1965

I said under my breath. "I would never trust the CIA."

Zane heard me, and then his voice took on a serious tone. "Are you ashamed of your father, Antonio Toscano?" he asked.

Startled by his comment, I clenched my fists, "What did you say?"

Zane wearing a grim look on his face said, "Kachada, your father was an OSS officer in France during World War Two."

"Tell me something I don't know," I said standing with both fists ready to strike.

Zane sat up, taunting me, and said, "Okay, try this. Your father, Antonio Toscano, worked as a highly classified CIA agent searching for those responsible for attacks against America." Then Zane went on to say, "And your dad didn't work only for your grandfather as a CPA. He was one of the original founders of the CIA in 1947."

My mind went into a whirl, recapping the mysterious events of my early life, *flipping cards like a time machine* when Zane gave me the final zinger. "That's right, Kachada, he was killed by terrorists. Terrorists he was hunting."

The revelation caused me to collapse into the wood chair by the hotel door. "What the fuck are you talking about?" I said in a haze.

Zane knew he had me now, and became more consoling. "Your dad was a hero to the CIA in Langley. One of those stars on the sacred wall . . ." He paused. " . . .is his."

"My mother told me when I was five that he died of a heart attack," I said staring at the floor in disbelief.

"Your mother only wanted to protect you." Zane stood up and walked over to me. "She knew about the CIA, but not what he was doing," he said.

My mind and face became blank as I recalled what my mother had said after she told me dad had died of heart attack, *"Trust no one, not even your mother."*

Zane broke my train of thought by placing his right hand on my shoulder and said, "When the CIA approached her to explain what happened, she knew you would be safer on the reservation." I gave Zane an emotionless stare, still processing all the information.

He continued, "She had a good reason to think they would come after you. They would have leveraged your life to get the names of other operatives your father worked with within the CIA. The CIA wasn't going to let that happen, and agreed with your mother's decision to send you to the reservation, where they could keep watch over you."

The dots were starting to connect, as I thought *about those two Military men she was arguing with after she told me dad had died.* This explained why Mom seemed so aloof.

Zane said compassionately, "When you were diagnosed with cancer, and given only two years to live, your mother had to let you go your own way. She knew the time had come for you to live the life you had left as you wished."

I was discovering mysteries *of my early childhood I never knew existed. I had to see my mother.*

Zane interrupted my thoughts. "I would like you to consider talking to me again."

"I can't make you that promise now," I said.

"You have a lot to digest. No promises. No one will know about this. To the CIA, you're the son of a hero who gave his life protecting his country. A true patriot," Zane said.

I asked, "How would I contact you?"

Zane said in CIA fashion, "You know how we work. You don't. I will contact you." He held out his hand. I needed more time, so I let his hand hang. "When you're ready," said Zane and walked out the door.

I paced the apartment, dissecting my childhood, my mother's distant affection—I was anxious to hear the truth from mom.

CHAPTER 16

December 12, 1975, Midtown Manhattan

I've always known my life was destined to be anything but normal. After my night with Zane, I realized how true that was. The Comanche believe every soul has a purpose. Knowing my father hunted the same beasts I realized I had been following in his footsteps. I needed to see Aponi and tell her everything I've discovered. I took the first flight to Atlanta the following morning.

Aponi encouraged me to tell my mother how much I loved her, knowing now what she gave up all those years to protect me. I flew to Pittsburgh and drove to Franklin to surprise my mother, and to find out more about dad.

I was sitting in a rented Porsche, listening to "Sittin' On The Dock Of The Bay," looking at my mother's house, when a yellow and black Camaro pulled next to me. At the wheel was a childhood friend. Nelson wound his window down and laughed, "I figured that was you! Who else would drive into this neighborhood with a fucking Porsche?"

I gave him the old neighborhood hello by flipping him the finger. Back when we were kids, I entrusted Nelson with all my secrets.

Nelson laughed and repaid the compliment, "What brings you to the exciting metropolis of Franklin?" he asked.

"I needed to see my mom. Been a while," I said.

Nelson informed me, "She works too many hours and looks tired, JT. I pick up her groceries now and then to help her out."

My mother's diabetes may be the problem. I thought. "Hey, man, I appreciate that, Nelson."

He nodded. "It's all good, man. Not a problem. You'd do the same for me." Nelson held up his infamous tiny amber bottle filled with what we called, in the day, "snow." He asked, "How 'bout a hit?"

"Like old times," I said and climbed into his Camaro.

Nelson warned me: "The cops still have a warrant out for your arrest. So I'd be careful not to let them find out you're in town."

"Those damn Reagle brothers," I muttered.

Nelson lets out a big infectious laugh. "Yep, you did a number on them. Ed still can't talk or eat real food?"

"He had the nerve to spit in my mother's face," I shouted.

"Well, I never see them around this area since you turned him into the village idiot." Nelson reminded me, "JT. Yep, you're still just trouble." Laughing. "How are you gonna get in without a key?" Nelson asked.

I held up my Swiss Army knife. "This is my key," I said.

Nelson said, "You always loved that weird knife. How many whatever's does it have?"

I spit out, "87 implements and 1,412 functions."

"JT, you're like some kind of fucking wizard. You know that? How long you in town?" Nelson asked.

"A couple days," I said.

"Touch base before you leave man," Nelson said.

"You know I will," I said. Even though we both knew I wouldn't. I got out of his Camaro and Nelson drove off. I walked up the four cracked cement steps to the large covered porch and sat on Grandpa's favorite swing, remembering *the evenings we would swing and he would tell me stories about coming to America.* I went to the door and jiggled my knife and slid my credit card between the door and frame. Open sesame.

I went directly to the kitchen and started making antipasto and linguini with red clam sauce for dinner. I located a bottle of Chianti and poured a glass as I waited for

Mom to arrive. I placed the pasta into one of Grandma's bowls she had brought from Sicily. I was spooning the homemade marinara when Mom opened the door —*Perfect timing*. She smelled the cooking and dropped her coat, running towards the kitchen, screaming my name. She squeezed me so hard she caught me off guard. That squeeze was worth the trip.

She pushed my long blonde locks off my face, "Why are you here?" Mom asked.

I didn't want to start with Dad. I wanted to enjoy this moment. "I miss you," I said.

Mom smiled, "You have pictures of Knoton and Aponi, right?"

I pulled out two wallet-sized four-color Polaroids. Mom took them and pulled me to the flowered print couch. She sat close to me, ooing and awing. "Kachada, he has your eyes, so clear and blue—and Aponi's thick black hair. You all look so happy."

I watched her every expression, savoring the moment, not wanting it to end. "I hope you're hungry," I said. "I made antipasto and linguine with red clam sauce."

She closed her eyes, "That smell hasn't been in this house since your last visit. Yes, very." I had the kitchen table already set. We sat down, to my delight, and began to reconnect.

I soaked up every luscious moment. Mom appeared to be tired and frail, more than I remembered. Her hair was turning gray and she wore her glasses all the time. I didn't ask about her health. I was afraid to hear her answer.

After finishing dinner, we sat in the living room. I delicately brought up Dad. Mom wasn't as taken aback as I expected. She asked, "Kachada, you spoke to someone?"

I began to tell her about Zane, the CIA and how I met the strange fellow Hayri she knew about. She sat patiently, listening to me, relaxing on the couch. Then she took my hand and began reliving her life as Mrs. Toscano, including the emotional details of Dad's death.

"Your dad worked endlessly to find those responsible for killing women and children in the south of France during the war. After he returned from the war, I could see he had seen the dark side of the world. He became obsessed with the brutality he had seen. I knew he was involved with the government. But I never knew specifics and I never asked.

"Then one night he confided in me, telling me he had information on a new terrorist organization developing in Syria. He told me the leader was someone connected to the horror he saw in France. I knew it had to be dangerous for him to mention it. I found myself thinking that I wish he wasn't telling me this. It made me worry more than I ever did before. Then it was only a few weeks later when two men in fine-looking suits came to the door. I didn't have to answer it to know why they came. I learned your dad had been working undercover with the CIA. They informed me Antonio was picked up in a van at gunpoint somewhere in Paris and was being held for ransom."

"For what?" I asked.

"They wanted the CIA to pay for his return. Your father had a photographic memory and remembered everything. His mind was a sponge. Nothing escaped it. He could recall anything at will. Something we learned you inherited. His head was filled with names, contacts, and covert missions the CIA could not allow to be revealed. Many of his friends' lives were connected to them."

"So what happened?" I asked.

"Your dad would never talk and paid the price. According to the information I was given, he was tortured for days. The terrorists finally gave up, knowing the CIA would not pay the ransom and killed him. The terrorists dropped his body in front of the U.S. Embassy in Paris."

"Is that why you took me to live with Grandpa Chief Peta?" I asked.

"The CIA was concerned the terrorists might try to retaliate, to prove they could reach across the ocean and strike at will. The CIA wanted us to change our names and move us to Canada. I refused, and insisted on taking you to the reservation. We argued till they finally agreed. I didn't want to waste a minute and left the next morning."

"Why didn't you take me to Grandpa Giovanni?" I asked.

"When your father died, I decided I wanted you to be raised as a Comanche warrior, knowing you would learn how to survive and learn about your Comanche heritage. It was important to me you learn the Comanche way while you were still a young boy. Your dad was as proud of his Sicilian ancestry as I am of mine. I told Grandpa Giovanni once you turned ten years old I would bring you to live with them. I knew you would be safe on the reservation and the Mafia would protect you while you were living with Grandpa Giovanni."

I saw Mom's pain at reliving Dad's death and felt so proud to be her son. I learned just how much my mom sacrificed to protect me. I learned the *truth.* My dad died a hero—not from a weak heart, but from a strong one.

Mom jumped up from the couch without warning and said, "I'll be right back." She returned holding a small cigar box. "Do you remember this?" Mom asked.

I recognized the Phillies Blunt Cigar box my dad gave me on my fourth birthday. "I do."

I opened it like a four-year-old and found the card.

Mom smiled. "You loved that card."

"Still do." I picked up my 1958 Mickey Mantle Topps Baseball Card. My favorite player," I said with a grin.

"You and dad loved baseball. Your dad loved the Pirates and you loved the Yankees. He got such a kick out of that," Mom chuckled.

We opened our hearts that night, making it a special time for her and for me.

The next morning Mom was gone. She left me a note on the kitchen table just like she did on my last visit.

> Kachada,
>
> Sorry but I am on my way to work. My brave son, you have a life to live with Aponi and Knoton. You never have to worry about me. Thank you for last night and have a safe trip home.
>
> Love, Mom

We had our mother and son day together. I would carry those hugs, kisses, tears, and memories of dad we shared forever. I put on "Blowin' In The Wind" and drove to the airport.

CHAPTER 17

December 18, 1975, LaGuardia Airport

While I was standing at the taxi stand at LaGuardia, a black SUV pulled up. The rear window rolled down. It was Zane. "Kachada. I'm your ride to the hotel." I hesitated before stepping into the back of the SUV. Zane asked, "Did your visit go well?"

I told him what he wanted to hear. "Zane, I learned my dad and I have much in common. Which is why I got into this SUV."

Zane opened the window between the driver and us and ordered him to drive to the agency. I became fixated on the images passing by as I looked out the blacked-out windows. I reached into my attaché and filled my pipe with hashish. "I need this," I told Zane.

Zane flipped open his Zippo and lit it. I inhaled the smoke and let it flow out slowly, gazing into cloudy swirls, sending me back to the reservation. *Sitting Indian style next to Kele, Chief Peta handed me the pipe. I held it and took a long puff. I held the smoke in until my eyes watered, releasing swirling clouds from my mouth.* The SUV stopped, bringing me back to Manhattan in front of the editorial building. "Why did you bring me here?" I asked.

Zane said, "You'll see." We continued to the alleyway and pulled up to a wall of Pennsylvania bluestone. It opened, revealing five parked black SUVs and an armed marine. He pressed a button, closing the wall behind us. It was like the opening sequence from *Get Smart.* Bright lights reflected off the polished cement floor. The room was lined with multiple heavy steel lockers that were loaded with an array of high-powered weapons. Zane signaled me to follow him. The guards hustled us into an elevator. The doors no sooner closed than they opened again, revealing a metal wall camouflaging the elevator.

The floor was made up of large white marble squares the ceilings were two stories high, with exposed steel beams throughout the entire open area. The interior glass walls were at least three inches thick, making them bulletproof, with no hidden views from one end of the floor to the other. I continued to follow Zane into a conference room. Black leather office chairs surrounded an oval mahogany table. A man in a black suit carried my favorite espresso with two lumps of natural sugar on a wood stirrer.

Zane sat down. "Kachada, I remembered how you enjoyed espressos at Cafe de Flore."

"Yes."

He didn't waste any time. "Kachada—or should I say JT?" Zane asked.

I took a sip of my espresso. "Only my friends call me JT. Kachada will do," I said.

Zane gave a half laugh. "Where do we begin?" he asked. I didn't say a word and took another sip of espresso. Zane waited for me to answer. But I didn't. "Okay, let's start when we first recognized you were a very dangerous man." As I listened, I scanned every inch of the space, gathering a series of snapshots, filing them away, including the five agents I saw on my way to the conference room.

Zane noticed me looking around and said, "Ah that brilliant brain of yours. Reminds me how dangerous you really are."

I finally answered, "Zane, get on with it, and get past this CIA bullshit."

"Listen, Kachada. Like you, I also lost family—my brothers. I witnessed them being killed by a small guerrilla group while on vacation in the Galapagos Islands. I can't bring them back, but I can get revenge for their death. I'm proud to say I spent the last ten of my thirty-one years hunting and doing everything I can to eliminate those murderers. So others don't have to live with the kind of horrible nightmares we do," said Zane.

"What if you're not telling me the truth? Prove you are who you say you are. After all, the CIA is famous for creating such fiction," I said.

Zane stood up and opened the thick glass door, signaling to the agent standing by. He turned and said, "I expected that, which is why I have a military AH-1 Cobra ready to fly us to Langley."

Wow, I didn't see that coming. "Right now?" I asked.

"Right now," he said holding the door open.

I always wanted to ride in an attack helicopter. "Let's go," I said.

It felt like we were floating along, ten thousand feet above cities, streets, and forests traveling at speeds over 277 miles an hour.

Once we landed on the CIA grounds we were greeted by Marines. Each gave us a salute. "Welcome to Langley, sir." Then they escorted us into the building.

Zane asked, "Well, Kachada, you enjoying this?"

"So far," I said calmly. *Inside I was screaming with excitement.*

We were being escorted through a series of elevators up to the third floor, where two suit-and-tie agents took over and led us to a private luxury suite that overlooked the compound. Zane left me in the suite with the two agents standing outside the glass doors. I sat waiting. He returned with a fresh pot of coffee. I was adding cream to my coffee when a man about five-foot-six inches or so, with a Greek nose, wearing unusually long dark brown hair, and kind brown eyes, walked in. He reminded me of Al Pacino in *Dog Day Afternoon*.

With one deliberate action, he shook my hand. "Kachada Toscano, I am honored to meet you, sir. I have seen your file. I am Director Panos."

Senator Wyatt quickly asked, "This is Director Panos we have no record of?"

"I don't know what you have, but he's the one I reported to," I said.

"Mr. Toscano. As we mentioned earlier, Director Panos is a mystery to us on this committee and to the DOD. Anything you can do to shed light on this so-called Director Panos would be much appreciated," said Senator Linkletter.

"And so I shall, Senators," I said.

When he told me he was the director I almost fell out of my seat. *This guy looked more like an undercover cop. Hearing the CIA had a file on me did not surprise me since the Delta flight.* I waited before I responded, then said, "I am honored to meet you, sir. But I'm not sure what's in your file."

Director Panos grinned. "A file of acts I consider nothing less than patriotic." Director Panos took a seat. "I understand you needed to clarify that Zane is who he said he is?" I nodded, sitting across from him. "We expected you would ask and you didn't disappoint us. Which is why I had an AH-1 Cobra ready. I wanted to meet you in person," Director Panos said.

"Why?"

There was a momentary pause. Then Director Panos said, "You have special talents you won't find in our training manuals at the CIA."

"What are you talking about?" I asked.

Director Panos unscrewed his water bottle cap from his Perrier and took a drink. He said, "For example, you have an IQ of 180. Can't teach that. You have a photographic memory. Can't teach that. You were raised as a Comanche Warrior and the Sicilian Mafia, quite a combination. Can't teach that either. And of course, there are your black belts in various Martial Arts. That we can teach. Then there is your father, Antonio Toscano, an OSS officer."

Director Panos sat down, put both hands on the table, and sat up straight, "You, Kachada, are one fucking dangerous person." I remained still, careful not to blink or give him any reaction. Then he said, "And JT, there are the 1,051,200 minutes. Yet here you are, still alive."

Calling me JT was another way of saying he knew everything. "Quite a mouthful, Director Panos," I said.

"Indeed it is, Kachada." He took another drink from his Perrier bottle and said, "Your country needs you."

"Why do you say that?" I asked.

"We have a growing crisis called terrorists. They are preaching their murderous prophecies to misguided souls who are joining their cause by the thousands. Causes like the one you witnessed on Delta 121. The terrorists you killed with your bare hands, thereby saving those one hundred and fifty passengers. To them, you are a hero. To me, you are a hero. A hero that could help us fight this battle to make this world safer from such horrible acts."

"Like my father, I love my country," I said.

Director Panos stood up and said, "Antonio Toscano's star is on our wall of fallen heroes who died protecting our country. You, Kachada, are the son of a hero who did a heroic act on that Delta flight. And now, because of that act, you are being hunted by the same terrorist groups responsible for killing your father."

I didn't want them to know they were right. "You don't know that."

Zane spoke up, "Isn't it true that there is a Comanche legacy that says, 'A Comanche warrior leaves no enemy alive.'"

I knew Zane was making a reference to Roses, Spain. But I kept silent.

Zane pulled the keyboard towards him and hit a button, projecting a young woman's headshot and docket onto the wall. He went into CIA briefing mode. "This is Vida Horvat from Izola, Slovenia, a small village on the coast of the Adriatic Sea, across from northeastern Italy." Zane turned to me and said, "Familiar?"

I kept a stoic face. He continued. "She's a graduate of the Academy of Dance at Ljubljana, was on tour in Damascus, Syria, at the age of nineteen. There she met Farid—*means unique*—Khan—son of Mohammad Khan, a terrorist responsible for organizing attacks since the early 50s throughout Central Asia and Europe. Farid is a member of the

Muslim Brotherhood, a radical group that has terrorized and killed many innocent people with homemade bombs. He converted her to his ideology a year before he organized the bloody FRAP shooting in Madrid," Zane said.

Director Panos and Zane waited for my response.

My head began spinning as replayed that day in Roses. *Vida wasn't an escort. How could I have been so fucking stupid?*

"Kachada," Director Panos said, "We've been following Farid since the Pan Am 707 bombing of December 1973. Our people were in Roses, Spain when Farid was found dead."

They knew I was there. I tried to throw them a curve and asked, "What does that have to do with me?"

"We can protect your family. The young woman at Roses was your only hiccup because you didn't follow your instincts," Zane said.

"We would like to work with you, together as a team. We would be there to protect your family," Director Panos said.

I stood up, raising my voice, "Director, are you using my family to threaten me?"

Director Panos, frustrated, took his hand away from his chin and pointed to the headshot of Vida. "*Vida Horvat.* She saw you and informed the ANO and they are now seeking revenge for you killing her *lover* Farid."

Zane jumped in and said, "We also know you're not working alone. One person could not locate targets that difficult to find without help."

I rubbed my hands across my face in frustration. I would not jeopardize Hayri's cover or his life. I needed to talk to Hayri before I did anything. My identity could be compromised because Abu got away and I let *Vida* live. Now my family could be in danger. My mind was whirling. "I need to think about this," I said.

"Okay, just remember you are the target of terrorists and that puts your family in danger," said Director Panos and left the room to Zane and me.

Zane said. "The AH-1 is waiting for us."

During the flight back, I couldn't believe Vida was working with a group of killers. I reviewed every detail of those twenty minutes in my head. I kept telling myself, *I should have killed her.*

I arrived back at the Paramount Hotel, exhausted, thinking about all the scenarios of how to find and kill Vida. I opened the hotel room door and heard, "Kachada."

Hayri was sitting in the soft leather chair. "Rough day?" he asked.

I was happy to see him and I blurted out, "Hayri, there is much to talk about."

"I know about Langley," Hayri said.

I thought, *of course; why else is he here? Why wouldn't he know about that? He's like a warrior who can smell blood across the oceans.* I asked, "How did you find out?"

"Because I also knew about Zane," Hayri said taking a sip of his Macallan.

Hayri must be some kind of wizard. "What? How—"

Hayri stopped me. "I wanted to see what they were up to and how far they would go to recruit you. If I were the CIA, I would go to any lengths. And that's the part that scares me."

"What do you mean?" I asked.

"Kachada, this is a dangerous game we're playing—the world's filled with twisted souls, twisted ideology, for all kind of twisted reasons. You are a son of a loyal patriot. Your ancestry fits their ideals and you have unique skills." He poured another glass of Macallan and handed it to me.

I held the scotch and sank into the dark espresso leather sofa, taking a sip. "Hayri, they suggested I left a woman alive who could target me, or worse, my family."

Hayri sighed. "Vida Horvat, from Izola, Slovenia." I looked guilty when Hayri said her name. *I never told him about leaving her alive.* Hayri scoffed, "Ask me how I know these things, Kachada."

"Because you know everything," I confessed.

Then Hayri surprised me. "Ah, that would be nice, but it's not true. I didn't know what the CIA wanted. But one of my sources told me she is alive in Damascus with Abu. And Abu knows about Roses."

I felt a queer feeling go over me and said, "Vida."

"But there is the good news. Vida did not see your face," Hayri said.

"But the CIA—."

Hayri interrupted me, "The CIA doesn't have that information. My thought is that they are playing you to convince you to join them. Kachada, understand, I don't trust the CIA, but they're right. They can protect your family. I cannot."

"Why is everyone telling me my family needs protection?" I complained.

Hayri said, "It's not just you, now. It's about finding these killers before they can do them harm."

A solemn and honest response I needed to hear. "Hayri, my dad was one of the original founders of the CIA. Terrorists killed him, not a heart attack."

"I know," he said with restraint.

I quizzed him, "Why didn't you tell me?"

"Your mother asked I not repeat that to you. I respected your mother's request. But since you now know, Hanni Naif, Abu's father, was responsible your dad's death," Hayri said.

"Abu's father, Hanni Naif, killed my dad? You're sure?" I asked, pressing my lips together and grinding my teeth as I heard Chief Peta. *Your ancestry has everything to do with your future.*

"The same ones who murdered my family. Yes, I am sure," Hayri said. "They are evil souls."

"How do I find Abu?" I asked.

"I know how you feel," Hayri said.

"I learned Vida was Farid's lover, not an escort. They've been together for years. I messed up and should have killed her in Roses," I said.

"That information is new," Hayri said. "I didn't know that."

"Do you think that's bullshit?" I asked.

"I told you I don't trust the CIA, and I wasn't sure what lengths they would go to bring you into their circle," Hayri said. "But you cannot take that chance." Hayri went quiet and then said, "Here is what I think you should do. I think you should join them."

"Because they can protect my family?"

"Yes, Kachada. Protect your family," Hayri said with a stern voice.

"What about you?" I asked.

He reminded me, "Kachada, I've been on this crusade long before we met."

I raise my glass and said, "You're a true friend. But I have a mess to clean up."

Hayri reached into the inside pocket of his brown wool jacket and handed me his business card with Vida's address written on it.

I took it and asked, "What if she didn't see me?"

Hayri, said without hesitation, "You can't take that chance. Besides, if the CIA is right about her, she's not innocent. That means she has killed in the name of Al Qaeda, and she will do so again."

I booked a flight to see my family in Atlanta before I started on my journey to kill Vida Horvat.

CHAPTER 18

January 5, 1976, Norcross, Georgia

Driving down River Bottom Drive past the lush entrance of Neeley Farms, weaving along the Chattahoochee River, I listened to the sounds of kids playing and the smell of southern pines.

I leaned forward, telling the driver, "It's the last house on the left of the cul de sac. Drop me in the driveway where the UPS truck is." The closest house sat thirty yards away, nestled among tall southern pines. I paid the driver and put my duffle bag over my shoulder. The UPS truck's engine was running.

I passed the overgrown pink pansies and said hello to our roaring cement lion protecting the house. I noticed the front door welcome wreath lying on the ground, and the door open. I picked up the wreath and stepped through the doorway.

To my horror, I saw a man attacking Aponi. I dropped everything and leaped into him, knocking him to the floor. Aponi got to her feet and ran. A blow to my forehead came from nowhere, knocking me down. Dazed, I saw a man dressed as a UPS deliveryman running after Aponi. He pulled her, tossing her into the wall. Fighting my cloudy head, I took a large clay pot and smashed it over the back of the man's head. Aponi lay bleeding. I turned to meet a pair of hands clutching my throat, dragging me to the ground.

Trying to shake off the cobwebs from the earlier blow, I brought my leg over his head and squeezed. I removed his grip, twisted his hand, and stood over him, turning his hand until I heard a bone snap. With my two-inch heel, I stomped my eel-skin cowboy boots into his throat until I smashed every human part in its path.

I started to go after the van, but it was gone. I turned my attention to Aponi. She was bleeding from her forehead and nose. "Aponi?" I said, holding her face.

She was delirious and pushed my hands away saying, "Knoton. In the den."

"Fuck." I ran through the doorway, pushing the rocking chair aside to get to his crib. My blue-eyed boy greeted me with a smile. I picked him up, hearing Aponi's feet behind me. She took Knoton from me, kissed him over and over then glanced up at me with blood dripping from her forehead. I felt helpless hearing Director Panos' voice, *"We would be there to protect your family."*

Aponi was hysterical. "Kachada, who were they? Why did they do this?" She asked me again and again.

I wrapped my arms around her. "I don't know," I said, thinking, *I know what I have to do.*

She pushed me away, and screamed, "Kachada. I want justice. No one fucks with our family. NO ONE!"

The front doorway was spotted with broken furniture, shattered pieces of pottery, and trails of blood from the doorway into the living room. The dead body of the attacker lay on the hardwood floor. What was once an image of a happy home was now the scene of a homicide. I hugged Aponi and Knoton thinking, *the reality of protecting my family is first and foremost.*

"Where are you going?" Aponi asked.

I gave her a kiss and said, "I need to call Zane." She knew who and what Zane was. I dialed the phone, looking out the kitchen window. The phone rang. *Pick up, damn it.* "Zane, I need to get to Langley. Yes, send a driver." I hung up and returned to Aponi.

"We belong on the reservation," Aponi said. I feel safer there."

I need to find Vida. "You're right. I'll let Kele know."

Fifteen minutes later, there was a knock at the door. "Kachada who is that?" Aponi asked.

"I have a driver coming," I said.

She shouted, "You just got here. I need you here. After all this, I need you here. We need you here."

It pained me to see her so frightened. I answered the door. A blonde burly man was standing in a suit and the traditional dark sunglasses. "Mr. Toscano?" He asked.

"Yes. I was expecting you," I said.

"Agent Czadankiewicz, sir. But just call me Tony. Much easier to pronounce," Agent Tony said with a handsome smile.

"Come in, Agent Tony. I said.

"Sir. Agents Getty and Watson will be here around the clock until you return," Agent Tony said.

"Stay here. I'll be right with you." I returned to Aponi and checked her forehead and nose. "You need a doctor," I said.

She pushed my hand away saying, "I'm fine. Who is that man?"

I turned and saw agent Tony, "Please bring your agents in here to meet my wife."

"Mrs. Toscano, I am agent Tony." He turned and gestured to the other agents and said, "Our agents will stay here to take care of you and your son while Mr. Toscano is away."

A slim curly-haired man with glasses said, "Hello ma'am, I'm Agent Getty and this is Agent Watson. We will take good care of you and your son."

Aponi reluctantly agreed, holding and kissing little Knoton. "Justice, Kachada. I want justice. Make it brutal," she demanded. The agents showed no emotion at her remarks.

I picked up my duffle bag and turned to agent Tony, "Let's go."

Hours later, I arrived at Langley on a private jet and was escorted to the familiar enclosed glass office where Zane was waiting. "Zane, they fucking attacked my family," I said.

"Are they okay?" Zane asked.

Pacing, I said, "Yes they'll be fine."

Zane said, "Kachada, let us help you. This is what we were afraid of. Let us help protect your family. These are dangerous people."

Even in this chaos, I didn't tell them I had Vida's address. "Where is she?" I asked.

Zane said, "Kachada, I cannot release that information without Director Panos' approval. Unless you were CIA."

I thought back to my conversation with Hayri and said, "I'm ready."

Zane tapped my shoulder and said, "I'll be right back."

Five minutes later, Zane returned and handed me a nine by twelve-inch manila envelope. I didn't waste any time opening it. I pulled the address from the envelope. Attached to it was confirmation booking me into the Beit Al Wali Hotel on Bab Touma Main Road under the cover name of Mike Fencik, a journalist working for Picasso Travel Agency. I thought, *How odd that they had this ready*. "Okay. How about the flight?" I asked.

"First I need you to sign this and we have a private jet waiting for you," Zane said.

I signed the document then started to leave and said, "Time to fix my mistake."

"I'm sending two more agents to your house. We'll also make sure Aponi and Knoton are safe and that Aponi sees a doctor," Zane shouted as the marine escorted me out.

I compared Zane and Hayri's source to see if they matched. They did. Vida was staying in a compound in Old Damascus, a neighborhood made up of bombed-out buildings among old hotels that were still operational. The compound was on Al-Qairmarryeh Street, where Vida was sharing space with other ANO and Al-Qaeda terrorists, according to the intelligence report.

At the hotel, long white curtains crashed onto the tan marble floor, blowing against hand-carved mahogany doors. The exquisite detailing throughout the room captivated me. Damascus was such a dangerous part of the world, yet the old world beauty of the hotel was a haven from it all. Still, I didn't come here to enjoy the detailing of the hotel. I came here to kill Vida Horvat. I drank tea and waited for the sun to rise. I dressed in wool pants and jacket with a crewneck jersey for the cool climate, which averaged sixty-three degrees year-round.

I walked the area and found Al-Qairmarryeh Street. It was a rough neighborhood; vigilance was a necessity when you wandered around in Old Damascus. I carried my journalist's ID with me in case the local police stopped me. The compound was made of stone and mud. The two-story building looked unstable, with battle scars from decades of conflict. The location and structure were going to be difficult to enter unnoticed.

I scouted the area for another possible access and found Café Al Bal. It sat on the end of the block south of the compound. Cafés in this part of the world were on every corner. Café Al Bal had signs of being under constant repair. New mud patches covered bullet holes. Cracks across the walls had been exposed from fallen tiles. The only light inside came from the street, through a patio exposed by a part of a blown-out wall. I ordered *kahwa,* a strong Turkish-style coffee served in tiny espresso cups. I patiently sat at the small iron table for two with a partial view of the street. Two hours passed as I read the *Al Baath,* one of the Damascus newspapers. I kept hearing Aponi say, *"Justice, I want justice. Make it brutal."*

I rubbed my hands together as I tried to warm them from the chilled air. Two older men arrived. One was carrying a small set of drums and the other a lute. They found a spot by the patio wall and started playing and singing poetic songs. I had heard about the poet-musicians. For outsiders like me, the image seemed strange. But these peaceful people were resilient, trying to live a normal life—among the terrorists who had infiltrated and brought so much death and destruction to their world. I listened and kept a watchful eye on the street activity as I fought the damp chill, with hopes of spotting Vida walking by. I waited long enough to not draw any attention to myself before I left the poet-musicians singing and returned to my hotel room. I decided I had to strike early in the morning. Knowing the difficulty that lay ahead of me, I had a hard time sleeping. I kept replaying the scene of Aponi bleeding on the floor.

DAY ONE

I returned to the café to give it one more try before the sunrise hoping I might find Vida there. It was a place of gathering for locals. But only two older gentlemen sat at a table. I wore the local baggy pants and a baggy shirt with a *keffiyeh* head wrap. If I were lucky enough to spot Vida, I would need to find a way to kill her outside the compound. If not, I had to risk going into the compound.

After two cups of kahwa, the sun began to break over the landscape. It was time. I left the café and stood near an alley across the street to focus on what I needed to do. I stepped further back into an alleyway, putting my silencer on. I inserted a clip, covering it with the *Al Baath* newspaper I brought with me from the hotel. I left three other clips in my left front vest pocket for easy access and took out my rosary. I rubbed it, praying for the souls Vida was responsible for killing.

I waited until the narrow street was nearly empty. The sun was starting to define the textures of the streetscape. There was no time to waste. I made myself mentally ready and had begun to cross the narrow street when I heard a voice say, *"Kachada."* I stopped. Just then, I was thrown onto my back, sending my Desert Eagle and keffiyeh into the street. I struggled to get up, wondering what had happened. My ears were ringing from the powerful explosion. Searching for my Desert Eagle, I turned to the compound. People were running out onto the street to see what had happened. It was mayhem, and the ringing in my ears blocked the street noise. Through the chaos, I saw the compound was flattened. Fire poured from it. The buildings next to the compound were left with skeletons of windows. The blast was devastating. Rubble covered the street. The locals seemed unfazed chattering as if they were attending a sporting event. The ringing in my ears was replaced by the sound of sirens.

I stepped on my Desert Eagle and quickly picked it up, and put it into my baggy pants, covered by my long vest. I was still wobbly, standing with others watching for the police to arrive. The voice I heard saved me from the powerful blast. *Perhaps Chief Peta was watching over me.* I waited to see if anyone came out alive.

The local police and firemen searched through the rubble and only carried two bodies. *Maybe Vida was one of them.* I waited for two hours. The crowd became disinterested and went on their way. I stepped closer to see if I could get a glimpse of the bodies. A policeman stopped me. I asked him, "Hal hnak 'ayu hayyat 'ukhraa?" *Are there any other bodies?*

"La. Faqat aljuthantayn alltyn jalabata." *No. Only the two bodies they brought out.*

Frustrated, knowing there was nothing more I could do, I left for the airport. My only hope was that Vida was one of the bodies they carried out. If not, I'd have to fly back to the states and regroup.

In the Damascus International Airport, I sat near a café waiting for my flight to London when a reporter on I Tele came on. I could see the small screen hanging by a metal pipe above the counter. A Parisian reporter stood outside the compound. A small crowd gathered around the tiny screen to hear what the reporter had to say.

> *Homemade bombs exploded and it's believed there were a number of ANO and Al Qaeda rebels inside. The blast leveled the compound, killing everyone inside.*

Hearing there were a number of people inside, my ears pricked up. It got even better when he said everyone inside was reported dead. *I could only hope that Vida was one of them.* They began showing grainy passport and driver's license photos of the identified fatalities. I anxiously bit my lip. I watched as a passport photo of Vida Horvat from Izola, Slovenia came on the screen. *Vida was dead.* I sat back, leaning against a divider wall, thinking *I can go home and tell Aponi that justice had been served.*

Then I couldn't believe my eyes. A passport photo of Sahi from the Skybar in Beirut appeared on the screen. Hayri and Zane were right. Sahi's photo confirmed Vida was connected to Abu. Proof she was a killer. After boarding the plane for the twenty-two-hour flight to Langley, I held my rosary, knowing in my heart it was my ancestors who warned me.

Two Marines escorted me to the conference room where Director Panos and Zane appeared to be having a heated discussion. Max, the massive young marine, signaled for me to stop. Max tapped the thick glass door and their tense faces turned to pretentious smiles as they waved me in. I had an odd feeling I had interrupted a discussion about me.

Director Panos said, “Kachada, good to see you. And good to see Vida was killed in that bast.”

I shook his hand and thanked him for all that the CIA had done.

Director Panos showed me a video they had of the reporter on I Tele displaying the pictures and names of those killed in the blast. “Kachada, you should know we dumped the body of Aponi’s attacker into a body bag and shipped him here, to Langley, to be identified,” Director Panos informed me.

“What about the one who got away?” I asked.

Zane said, “We tracked the UPS truck he was driving to a small airport hangar in Dekalb, Georgia, a town not far from Neeley Farms. He got into a gunfire battle with our agents. He lost.”

Director Panos said, “From what we can tell, it looks as though they were part of the Yugoslav terrorist group.”

Surprised, I asked, “Why would a Yugoslav terrorist group attack my family?”

Director Panos replied, "Vida Horvat was tied to them through Farid." It seemed odd to me, but I didn't question him knowing how terrorist groups are spread throughout Eastern Europe and Central Asia.

Director Panos said, "I am told I can call you Agent Toscano."

Without hesitation, I squeezed his hand. "Yes, Abu is still alive. I am committed to finding him."

Director Panos smiled. "I am going to leave agent Toscano with you, Zane. Now I can enjoy lunch knowing you are one of us. Zane, take care of our prize."

Zane said, "You know I will." Director Panos left with a marine escort. Zane and I got right to work planning our next move before I flew back to Atlanta.

CHAPTER 19

February 14, 1976,
Norcross, Georgia

It was Valentine's Day, oddly enough; the sound of my footsteps on the empty hardwood floor was disheartening. I finished checking the rooms and stood in the empty loneliness of our once happy home. The moving truck was to arrive at the reservation the next day. Before I locked the front door, I turned, *seeing Aponi painting it black, taking great care not to get any paint on the cement lion.* I gave the loyal cement lion a pat and said goodbye. The blacktop street was still black in color, framed by crisp white sidewalks. I rolled down the windows and looked out the windshield of my BMW, wishing Knoton could have grown up here. I cranked up Janis Joplin's "Piece Of My Heart" on my stereo, and took one last tour of River Bottom Drive, passing kids playing and families going about the business of living out their American dream.

Aponi and I enjoyed the simple life on the reservation as husband and wife, mother and father. Every day we further removed ourselves from the ugly memories in Atlanta. I needed to take the time and kept my distance from Zane and Hayri. We rode horses every morning to the mountain to watch the sunrise and every evening to watch the sunset. It became our family ritual to connect to our Comanche ancestors.

I experimented with different natural herbs I found on the reservation, mixing them to find the best combinations for energy. I started a routine of running in the mornings after my martial arts workouts. This helped to keep my leg from becoming stiff while I focused on my purpose, to find Abu.

One morning after my run, Aponi held me close and whispered in my ear, "I love you, but you need to go."

I didn't expect to hear that. "Why?" I asked.

"You are here but your spirit is not. You have done all you can here. Knoton and I are safe here. Go find Abu. Then we can once again be a family. We will be here waiting for you."

I knew Aponi was right. The next morning I kissed Aponi and Knoton goodbye and made arrangements with Zane to fly New York City.

"Enjoying the view?" Zane asked.

"Quite a view," I said standing on the 103rd floor of the World Trade Center looking over the Hudson.

"I never get tired of it," Said Zane.

"Propaganda Marketing and Production Agency?" I asked.

Zane, admiring the view, said, "Kachada, my friend, it's the name of our company."

"*Our company?* I don't remember starting one," I said.

With a laugh, Zane said, "We didn't want you to waste that Journalism degree."

My sarcastic reply, "How considerate."

Zane shook my shoulder and said, "It's the advantage of being employed by the DOD. They start it for you. No money, no credit checks or paperwork required."

I asked the obvious, "Any clients?"

"Yes, one. Follow me," Zane said. "We've been building the company with state-of-the-art production equipment. We dressed it up to give Propaganda that creative vibe. What do you think?"

"Impressive."

"There's more." Zane started the tour. "I had it designed with hidden security rooms and weapon closets incorporated into the space. Look at this." He pressed a button and a wall-sized projection board covered the wall of Andy Warhol prints. "Sexy." The environment oozed with a creative lure. "And of course, as you have seen, the coup de grâs." We looked through the floor to ceiling windows at the awe-inspiring view of the city on our way to the conference rooms with multiple TVs." They formed one large wall of screens. "And here is our culinary kitchen any James Beard award-winning chef would envy."

"Damn impressive," I admitted.

"And here's the most important part," Zane revealed a wet bar behind a turn-style wall, filled with top-shelf liquor. I followed him through two large, hand-carved wooden doors. "Meet our five-star hotel suites." The suites could compete with the ten thousand dollar a night suite at a suite in the Geneva Hotel.

"This is truly sick," I said.

Zane said with pride, "I know. I wanted to do it right."

Are these for clients?"

"For us." Zane laughed, "This way we can keep a low profile while living in the city. If anything is missing, just let Joanne know. I will make sure you have what you need."

"Who is Joanne?" I asked.

"See that great-looking agent at the front desk?" Zane asked.

"Agent?" I asked.

Zane said, "You, me and Joanne, are Propaganda."

I pressed him about Joanne. "She CIA?"

"She is on loan from the Mossad and is here to keep tabs on us for Langley," Zane said. "And get this. She has an identical twin. Both were trained by the Mossad."

I gave her a more respectful glance. "The *Mossad*?"

Zane walked over to the long wooden conference table and handed me a brochure.

"What is this?" I asked.

"You asked if we had any clients," Zane said.

"A Chinese technology company?" I asked.

Zane scoffed, "Not just any Chinese technology company. One with offices in Saigon,

Seoul, Shanghai, London, Prague, New York City, and your favorite: Paris."

"How…?"

Before I could finish my question Zane held up his hand and shook his head. "Don't ask. I don't. We have a research company provided by the DOD looking for brands with an international marketing budget. They make the contact and voila. We have a client." Then he asked, "Hey, what do you say we go to Palm Too for dinner? We'll celebrate your return to New York."

"Palm Too. Works for me," I said, delighted by the thought.

Zane glanced over to Joanne. "Joanne, can you make reservations for Kachada and me at Palm Too tonight. Around—what?" He turned to me. I suggest 8 p.m. Zane repeated, "Make it for two at 8:00 p.m."

Zane left and I claimed one of the hotel suites, unpacked, and showered before going to dinner. Joanne was going over data as I walked to the elevator. I asked, "Don't you take time off?"

She gave me a beautiful smile. "I don't know if you heard, JT, but there are bad guys we need to find."

I liked her sense of humor.

My driver dropped me at 840 32nd Avenue, in front of the Palm Too. Caricatures of famous patrons covered the walls among the dark oak and white tablecloth setting.

The maître d' asked, "Mr. Toscano?"

"Yes," thinking, *I'm impressed he knows who I am.*

"Please follow me," he said. We arrived at a secluded table in the corner by the front window. Zane was wearing a t-shirt, dark blue Yves St. Laurent Jacket, and black jeans. He gave me his pearly-white smile and poured me a glass of 1875 Chateau Laffite Rothschild setting on the table.

The waiter, wearing the traditional white jacket and black bowtie attached to a starched tuxedo shirt, magically emerged with an appetizer. “Mr. Kendrick, your Carpaccio of beef tenderloin with arugula, lemon, black pepper, olive oil, and shaved parmigiana Reggiano. Is there anything else I can bring you?”

Zane was in his element. “Thank you, Toma. Please give us a couple of minutes to look the menu over,” Zane said. “We live well because it could be our last meal.” We raised our glasses. “To Propaganda.”

Zane asked, “What do you think about the setup?”

“Hard to believe what it must have cost for the space alone,” I replied.

“Kachada, you will find money will be no object for us. Our operation is seen as a critical component in fighting our enemies,” Zane said.

The waiter returned for our entrée order. Zane asked, “Kachada?”

I said, “I’ll start with the Caesar salad. Then I’ll have the double cut lamb chops with wild mushrooms and goat cheese whipped potatoes. Please.” Then Zane ordered the lobster bisque and the house special.

We finished the Carpaccio appetizer, admiring the caricatures covering the walls. I jested. "Do you think a restaurant exists somewhere in Syria with caricatures of terrorists adorning their walls?"

Zane caught off guard, laughed. "If it were only that easy."

We ate dinner, discussing the Propaganda covert strategy. I asked Zane, "Why did you call it Propaganda?"

He explained, "Propaganda has an international flair, allowing us to place an office somewhere in Europe or Eastern Europe."

"Have you decided where?" I asked.

"It's between Prague and Paris," Zane said finishing up the last of his lobster bisque.

I snickered. "Let's see, you have Paris, France, and the Paris of Eastern Europe, Prague."

Zane said. "Yes, and we need to open it soon. For the Sung account."

"Yes, the Chinese company. How did a Chinese company buy into a company based in the States?"

Zane reminded me, "They bought into a company based in either Prague or Paris. Which is why the decision needs to be made soon."

Curious, I asked, "Why them?"

"We were looking for clients promoting new avenues in the technology sector. It allows us to access new tech products, and then hand them off to our FBI brothers. They then analyze the new technology."

I was surprised by his answer. "They're smart people. Why would they trust any company to take their products outside of their watch?" I asked.

Zane responded with, "There is technology in Europe we have and they don't. Combining their breakthroughs and forming partnerships across Europe could launch them as a world leader in the technology business sector. They're masters at stealing other's technical data. They could then use it to influence their political standing in the world, which would mean more international clout. And the real advantage would give us the freedom to cross the borders as their marketing agency to countries where terrorist cells are hiding."

I posed the hard question: "So what happens when they find out Propaganda is a front for the CIA?"

Zane continued in a cutting tone. "First, we won't let that happen. Second, if they do, it becomes a coup for us, having collected top-level information they would be too embarrassed to publicly admit we had. And third, we are not officially the CIA." Zane quickly changed the subject. "Now, what do you think of Joanne?"

Reeling from his statement, I asked, "Whoa, back up. What do you mean we're not CIA?"

Zane leaned in, speaking in a quiet voice, "We operate under our own rules. Director Panos is not CIA."

"He shook my hand and said welcome to the CIA," I said.

"We use the CIA facilities as a front when needed, but he was appointed by a high-level cabinet member to run Propaganda outside the CIA's political thumb," Zane said.

"We had CIA agents at my house after the attack, and agents at Langley escorting us to offices in the CIA. And your ID badge you showed me at the hotel. Doesn't seem very autonomous," I said.

Zane said, "All they know is we're a special group with special privileges given the resources we need from other departments. They don't know the details of what we do. Nor do they want to know. They do what they are told and that is all. That gives us access to anything the CIA has to keep us from being identified as a lone wolf operation top-level politicians and committees in D.C."

"Are you talking about the Senate Select Committee on Intelligence? The President?"

"I didn't say that. Nor do I want to know. Let's leave it at that," Zane said as he drank the last of the 1875 Chateau Laffite Rothschild.

"Okay. So whomever the hell I am working for all I really care about is finding Abu. That's why I'm here. If all that other bullshit helps, then I'm happy. What's on tomorrow's agenda?" I said.

"Abu," Zane said.

I replied, "Music to my ears."

"He is one of our main targets. I'm flying to Langley first thing in the morning for the next steps on choosing the city for the European Office," Zane said.

I offered, "My two cents is Paris."

Zane laughed, "Why am I not surprised."

A month later, Joanne was working with Langley to identify targets. Zane was spending most of his time in our Prague office to find and hire a staff to handle the daily business needs. Joanne and I ran the satellite office in New York, writing and creating promotions for Propaganda's clients.

Aponi's modeling career had become star status. Europe had become fascinated by Aponi's Native American look, making them her biggest fans. She had become constantly booked for photo shoots. Her latest booking was in New York for the upcoming French, Spanish and German *Elle* Covers and was staying with me at the office suite. After a long day of filming, we toasted her trip with a bottle of Dom Perignon, admiring the 103rd-floor view of the city lights.

"I never get tired of the view," Aponi said.

"Maybe you and Knoton should move to the city?" I suggested.

"I love visiting," she said, crushing any thoughts of her and Knoton joining me in Manhattan.

I confessed, "I count every minute when I'm away from you and Knoton."

"You are with us every one of those minutes." We snuggled back onto the large leather couch, sipping Dom, and turned our attention to each other and back to the spectacular view.

CHAPTER 20

April 10, 1976, 103rd floor,
South Tower, World Trade Center

I had finished my morning coffee and noticed Aponi and Joanne were having a serious conversation. I interrupted asking, "Everything okay?"

Aponi quickly stopped and replied, "Just fine." She gave me a kiss goodbye. The elevator doors opened and Zane darted out, bumping into Aponi. In a haste, he asked, "Aponi, did your photo shoot go well?

"Very well," she said giving Joanne a wave as the elevator doors covered her smile.

I turned to Joanne and asked, "What's that all about."

Then an excited Zane said, "We found our target; let's meet in the conference room," and scurried off. We followed him and sat down. Immediately he started punching in data, bringing up a series of images over the wall-sized screens. We gathered around the table. "This is Nisar Uzza, aka Fadi Nour, leader and co-founder of the secular nationalist party Fatah, a top aide of PLO's Chairman Yasser Arafat, and commander of Fatah's armed wing, Al-Assifa. He is connected to a part of the Tel Aviv attack during the high holy days," Zane said without taking a breath.

Joanne focused in on one image. Zane did as well and paused. "Joanne and her sister Suzanne watched Nisar kill their family," Zane said.

Joanne remained still, not saying a word. Zane continued, "He coordinated the gunning down of twenty innocent passengers and the injuries of one hundred twenty others during the Pakistani Army siege. It is also believed he planned Abu Naif's hijacking of Pan Am Flight 73."

"Abu," I unconsciously blurted out.

Zane paused watching Joanne's face focused on Nisar. Then Zane said, "And now he's believed to be planning an attack with Abu on Brussels. Our intelligence tells us he is in Tunisia now."

I asked, "So you think Abu is with him?"

"Yes," Zane replied.

Joanne asked, "Dead not alive. Right?"

"Right," Zane said. "Let's go over how we do that."

It was obvious to me that Joanne was on a mission no different than mine. We both had scores to settle with these terrorists. Which explained why the Mossad loaned her to our team.

After a long night going over our strategy on how to take out Nisar Uzza, I was up early doing my morning martial arts exercises with Abu on my mind. The thought of finding him pushed me through the pain of my routine. Afterward, I took the Wall Street subway to 49th Street. Holding on to the railing, I thought *about Joanne's face when she saw Nisar.* We stopped at Bay Ridge and I noticed a young girl straggling behind a forty-something man, with long curly sidelocks known as payots under a black bowl hat.

I was envisioning a Reuben sandwich when I heard the man say, "Geyn tsu di tsurik." *Go to the back, in Yiddish.* He pointed towards the back of the train car. The girl obeyed him like a dog would his master.

Shaking my head, I whispered, *"Asshole."* He glanced up and I reminded myself not to get involved. I rode to the 49th Street stop and started walking to 47th. The Hasidic Jew passed me at a fast pace, shouting, "Hurry up." The young woman was struggling to keep up. At that moment I realized the young girl, all of seventeen or so, was his wife.

I ignored what I heard and pictured *my hot Reuben filled with corned beef, Swiss cheese, sauerkraut, Russian dressing on dark rye bread.*

I left the husband continuing to berate his young wife, barking at her, when I arrived at Andy's Deli. I found an empty table next to a pair of lovely women of fifty or so. One of the lovely ladies called the waitress over. "Hello dear, what is your name?"

The waitress replied, "Sarah ma'am, and you?"

"Harriet. You are a very sweet girl, but my soup is cold," Harriet said.

The waitress was flustered. "So sorry, I'll take care of it and return in just a few minutes, ma'am."

Harriet leaned towards me. "Can you believe they brought me cold soup? They charge five dollars for cold soup. That's ridiculous." Then she asked me, "What's your name, young man?"

I smiled and said, "Kachada, ma'am."

She moved her chair closer. "That's an odd name. My name is Harriet. My, my, those clear blue eyes of yours. It's as though they can see right through me," Harriet said.

I teased her and said, "Because they can."

"What do they see?" she asked with a flirty smile.

I moved closer to her face, looking into her eyes, and said, "A lovely woman who deserves her soup to be served hot."

She let out a belly laugh and said, "Aren't you a sweetie? You married?"

"Yes. Why do you ask?"

"Oh, what a shame. My twin daughters don't seem to be doing well enough on their own, so I'm always looking to help them out," Harriet said.

I chuckled. "Sorry, Harriet. I can't help you with that."

"Enjoy your Reuben," Harriet said turning her attention to the arriving bowl of hot soup.

The sidewalks were bustling when I left Andy's. The street had become one big traffic jam of cabs and delivery trucks. New York City was more than just a city to me—it was an energy I had become addicted to.

On my way to the office, I recognized the young girl-wife from the subway train. She was standing out in front of a jewelry store, shivering. Her posture was slouched, like a child being punished, and her head was staring down at the cold sidewalk. Her sad posture reminded me of an article I read a couple of years earlier in the New York Times about a Hasidic wife who was forbidden to talk to or look at anyone outside of her community. I gave her a polite smile as I walked by. Her husband was inside, nice and warm, cleaning the glass cases. I kept on walking for about half a block and stopped. I turned to see the cold, mistreated young wife, thinking, *He's treating her like an animal.* I waited for a moment longer and kept walking for about another half block. I couldn't get her sad face out of my head.

I recalled the name of the organization and stopped. I took out my Propaganda business card, emblazoned *Kachada Toscano, North American Executive Creative Director* and scratched the name and phone number of the place I remembered from the article on it. I went into a fast-walk thinking, *she could choose to call the number or not.*

When I approached, her sparkly blue eyes danced in my direction. She kept her head facing down. I pretended to be looking at the diamond arrangements inside as I bent down, looking at the merchandise. I held the card with my left hand below the glass window as I held my right hand up to my face, pressed against the storefront window, pretending to admire the merchandise. I didn't want her husband to see me handing her the card. She did nothing. I spoke Yiddish facing the glass storefront window and pushed the card towards her hand and said, "These people can help you."

She didn't respond. I began to pull the card away, thinking *I overstepped my bounds* when her left hand struck the card like a cobra. She tucked it under the palm of her hand, covering it with her long-sleeved jacket. She never once changed her obedient posture, looking only toward the sidewalk.

Her husband poked his head out asking, "Can I help you?"

I turned to him and asked, "Do you make custom jewelry?"

His face lit up and said, "Why, yes. We are known for our custom designs. Would you like to come in?"

I glanced at the girl and said, "I wasn't going to stop because of the vagrant standing in front."

He turned to her and barked, "Nava, — *beautiful* in Yiddish—go inside and stop scaring my customers away."

"I'm sorry," he said, "She can be a nuisance. Please come in." I caught myself staring at him thinking, *you prick.* Nava obeyed and scurried to the back, continuing to stare at the floor. "Can you tell me what you are looking for?" he asked.

"My wife is Aponi," I said. "I want to surprise her."

His eyes blew up to the size of quarters. "Aponi the supermodel?"

"So you've heard of her?" I asked.

He babbled on, "Yes. Yes. She is one of the most beautiful women in the world. I would be honored to design a custom piece for such a jewel."

"I was just looking. Do you have a card?" I asked.

"Yes, of course, I am Velvel Yossi." He handed me his card and said, "I will design a very special piece for your beautiful wife. And what is your name?" Velvel asked.

"Kachada. Kachada Toscano," I said.

"Comanche like Aponi?" He asked with a geek smile.

I stared at his yellow teeth, thinking *you pig*. I turned, never answering him, and walked out feeling better than when I walked in knowing Nava was out of the cold.

CHAPTER 21

June 6, 1976, 103rd floor, South Tower, World Trade Center

While I was mixing another concoction of herbs, plant root, with skim milk, Zane came running in carrying his leather folder. "Let's meet," he shouted. Joanne followed from the front desk and I brought my drink, meeting them in the conference room.

The wall came alive with images of Nisar and streets with circles on them. Zane went into his briefing voice. "Okay, we now know for certain Nisar Uzza is in Tunis, living with a small group of terrorists, along with Abu Naif."

Joanne and I kept our silence.

Zane went on, "As you know, they are responsible for a list of horrific acts, including the 1972 Munich Massacre, and the 1974 bombing of TWA Flight 841."

Hearing Abu was part of this mission gave Joanne and me hope that we could have our revenge.

Zane said, "We don't know exactly who the others are. But we believe they are all high-level members of Al Qaeda. Our plan is to pose as the Mossad." Zane caught his second breath. "We do know the terrorists sleep during the day and roam at night. So we need to be prepared for total darkness once inside the three-floor villa. Nisar will be upstairs. He is a man of habits. He always takes the top floor wherever he stays. The second floor is the kitchen." Zane pointed to the circles over the villa. "The first floor we believe is a bedroom and bathroom. When we arrive, a van with a driver will be parked in front." Zane circled the street front. "He will be ready to whisk them off at any given moment."

"I want Nisar," Joanne ordered.

"Yes, I know. You will take the third floor and I'll take the driver in the van. The entrance is on the second floor. Kachada, you immediately take the first floor." Zane scratched our names over the floors. "If everything goes as planned, we walk out and return to our hotel and catch the next flight to Paris."

"And if not?" I asked.

Zane put down his orange grease pencil and said, "We will take the van. Our intelligence in the area will contact a Navy base in Capodichino and send a SEAL team to meet us at Carthage, a small village off the Gulf of Tunis. There, the SEAL team will escort us to Marsala. A private jet will then fly us to Capodichino and then to Paris the next day."

"Sounds easier than it looks," I said.

Joanne replied. "Whatever it takes to get Nisar." I nodded my head in agreement.

Zane said, "We all know no mission is ever easy. A private jet will be ready to take us tomorrow morning" and left.

We checked into the Ibis Hotel, four miles from the airport. After reviewing our plan, I took a walk and found a local restaurant around the corner. I ordered a plate of steamed mussels in a garlic and butter sauce with couscous and Kersa bread. It reminded me that the bombed-out buildings didn't define these people. Their rich heritage of foods and friendly spirit did.

From the front seat of an old Volvo, I secured the silencer to my Desert Eagle watching our target's location. We were dressed as locals, wearing Sirouel *baggy trousers,* a Montane *a vest style jacket,* and a round felt hat called a Chedhia. We waited in silence for the first sign of dawn.

"There's the van," Zane said. A powder blue VW van drove up and parked in front. Two men got out and entered the villa. "Those two should make six inside," Zane informed us. The driver of the van relaxed his head back on the seat's headrest. "Remember, speak

Hebrew." The only sounds were us loading our weapons and the rustling of our clothes. "Let's go," Zane ordered.

I was the first to step out, with Joanne beside me. Zane followed and signaled for us to hold. He walked up to the van. He reached through the open window and snatched the man's head, and before he could make a sound, slit his throat. After the quiet kill, we crossed the street and moved to the alleyway door. Zane opened the unlocked door and entered. Joanne and I were right behind him. It was black inside. We pulled our night goggles down. We heard a growling noise and suddenly, a Malinois dog attacked Zane, knocking him down. Then the mayhem began.

The house lights flashed on. The white light blinded me. I pulled off my night goggles in time to see Joanne popping two shots into the dog. I adjusted my vision. Joanne turned and ran to the third floor. Zane was back on his feet. Gunfire from the second floor pinned Zane down as I heard Joanne's silencer popping upstairs.

"Kachada, get to the first floor," Zane shouted in Hebrew.

I jumped down the flight of stairs. Greeting me was the sound of a Russian made APS automatic, ripping through the wall. Bullets ricocheted upstairs from intense gunfire. My instincts were to join them, but I had my assignment. With a pause in gunfire and the sound of reloading, I rolled to the opposite wall. A large image of a man swung a Syrian sword catching the barrel of my Desert Eagle. I slid to my right, ducking from the attacker and popped him with four rounds. He fell directly on top of me, taking another round of gunfire from an open doorway.

The sound of an older voice screamed in Arabic, "Stay here." It signaled to me there was more than one person behind the open doorway. I heard scraping sounds of metal across the cement floor. I pushed the dead man who was staring into my eyes aside and took his APS. I shot several rounds into the area the gunfire came from. I heard the small sounds of whimpers, then it became quiet, I crawled cautiously to the opening. My leg became numb. I braced myself and rolled past the opening and into the room, holding the APS ready to take fire.

I bit my lip and tried not to lose my mind. A metal bed frame was sitting on its side. Trapped behind it were three young children, riddled with bullet wounds. Hiding behind them was an older man trying to reach his Russian made Makarov pistol that was lying just out of his reach. I managed to stand up, staring at the young bodies he'd used as a bulletproof barrier. The children hadn't stopped all the bullets. One of his shoulders was blown off, leaving him only one good arm and two shots to his stomach. In the room, there was a video set up with dried bloodstains on the floor. He didn't say a word.

I looked down at the dead children then back to his face. He had no expression. The room had tools used for torture. I knew then this was an execution room. Above me, the gunfire had all but stopped. I pulled the bed away and placed the children's bodies side by side. I turned, and in one wicked move, I shoved a grenade into the man's mouth. I leaned close to his face and said in Arabic, "Kiss your ass goodbye." Then I pulled the pin and leaped to the other side, feeling the blast tossing rubble onto my back. I looked over my shoulder to an empty black hole where the man once was. The bodies of the children were covered but not blown up. I started to uncover them when I heard Zane.

"Kachada. You okay?" Zane asked, running down the stairs.

"That bastard used those little kids as his bulletproof vest," I said looking down at what was left of the young bodies. Then I noticed Zane was bleeding through a cloth wrapped around his leg. "Zane, you hit?" I said.

"Just a knife wound. They dead? Did you see their faces?" He asked.

"Yes. None of them were Nisar or Abu," I said.

"Let's go."

I started to move more rubble from the children's bodies when Zane said, "We have to go. You have to leave them. I took out my rosary and said a silent prayer and then followed him, hobbling up the steps.

Joanne came from the third floor, covered in blood from her chin to her boots.

"Joanne!" Zane called out.

"Their blood, not mine," she said. Then she shouted, "No, Nisar."

We wasted no time and ran to the van. The street had attracted a crowd of onlookers. Zane raised his Desert Eagle and screamed, "Get back," in Hebrew. They stepped aside. I dumped the dead driver and started the van. Zane and Joanne pointed their weapons at the crowd and climbed in.

Zane screamed in Hebrew, "Go."

Leaving dust and dirt behind, we raced down the narrow street, chased by a crowd throwing rocks and whatever they could find. A bullet struck the back window as I turned the corner, shattering glass onto Joanne. "Keep going, I'm not hit," she screamed.

Weaving through the street, Zane ordered, "Take that right. Now go down that road and don't stop." We bounced down an even narrower alleyway into a rebel green military Jeep. Five men with weapons pointed at us and forced me to stop.

"Say nothing," Zane whispered. A tall man wearing a black beret came up to my window. We stared, not saying a word. Our bodies were covered with blood and dirt. He walked to the back window, signaling for Joanne to wind it down. I watched in the rear-view mirror. She didn't take her eyes off of him.

"Go," Joanne shouted. I put the pedal to the metal, watching the other four hold their fire as I pushed past the Jeep. Joanne had her belt wrapped around the man's neck, holding his head inside the van to protect us as we speed down the rough road.

Zane screamed, "Faster." I pushed the pedal to the floor, dragging the soldier's feet. The man was crying in pain, fighting to get loose. His feet were turning into bloody stumps.

Joanne was determined not to let him go. "Keep going," she ordered.

I drove for two more miles. When I heard a pop from Joanne's silencer. The soldier's body rolled along the ground. I kept driving. "Where to?" I shouted to Zane.

"Stay on this road," Zane said. I drove through nightfall until a row of bright lights forced me to stop. Four Navy SEALs signaled for us to get out. We followed to a Navy Rigid Hull Inflatable Boat they called a RIB. We climbed into the inflatable jet boat and raced across the Mediterranean to Marsala. None of us said a word.

The sun was rising when I crawled out of the chopper at Capodichino's naval base. Joanne stepped out, carrying her Desert Eagle by her side, with dried blood still covering her from her chin to her boots. I helped Zane hobble with his leg wrapped in a blood-soaked cloth. I had spots of dried blood on my chest and face. We looked like a scene from a Quentin Tarantino movie. The SEALs escorted us to the barracks as others military men and women stood by watching.

"Not a word about this to anyone," Zane ordered. I dropped onto a bunk and closed my eyes, *seeing the dead eyes of three innocent children.*

"Kachada. Wake up." Zane was rocking me shouting.

"What the F...."

"Come on. Take a shower. Our plane has arrived," Zane said.

Standing under the hot spray of water, I watched the dried blood turn liquid, circling the drain. In the next stall, Joanne was showering off her frustration. She glanced over and sighed. "Fucker wasn't there." Then turned away.

After drinking one of my concoctions of roots and coffee grounds from the *Rubiaceae* family, I walked into the lobby. My leg was feeling good and I hadn't said a word to anyone about the numbness episode in Tunis. Joanne hadn't arrived yet. The New York Times was lying on her desk. I picked it up and headed for the conference room. I perched on a table, flipping through the sections, as the sun was lighting up the Manhattan skyline. I heard Joanne walk in, apologizing, "I'm sorry, I got caught in the traffic jam coming in from the Hamptons."

"Hey, it's fine. Are you okay?" I asked reading the *Times*.

"Waiting is not something I enjoy," she scowled settling in at her desk.

Since our frustrating withdrawal from Tunis, we'd been on edge, waiting for the call on Nisar. I ambled into my office, leafing through the paper. I turned to the front page of the city section and stopped in my tracks. It was spread across the front page. A picture of Nava was above the headline:

> Woman Commits Suicide Outside
> of Life Savers

My heart dropped as I read:

> Nava Yossi's body was discovered lying in the cold outside of Life Savers in Brooklyn. She suffered a fatal head wound from a small-caliber pistol. Life Savers is the only nonprofit organization that provides educational, vocational, and social support to people who leave their communities. Mrs. Yossi left Bushwick, Brooklyn in January after a stranger encouraged her to reach out for help and gave her our name and number said Slana Krindler.

Those bright blue eyes, looking so hopeless. I read on:

> Slana, one of the counselors at Life Savers, reported Nava had been sent threatening letters stating, 'We have a headstone waiting to bury you in the ground, where you belong.' According to Krindler, 'This represented one of many threatening letters Nava received. It's hard to face the world once

> you leave a community, even after you realize you don't have to be subjected to the abuse anymore. Nada, who was only seventeen years old and had been forced to marry a man more than twice her age, could not make the adjustment and chose to leave this world instead of living alone in it.' When we approached her estranged husband, his only comment was 'God didn't want her, but the devil did.'

I put the article down thinking, *my card caused her death.* Joanne noticed that I was distraught.

"What's wrong?" She walked over and picked up the paper. "Do you know this Nava?" she asked.

Looking straight ahead, I said, "Yes."

Joanne continued reading the article. "You gave her the number?" Joanne asked.

I muttered, "I shouldn't have gotten involved."

Joanne sat next to me and said, "I've seen this before. This would have happened with or without you." She leaned towards me and whispered, "A damn good beating is necessary." Then got up, turning to me, and said, "Don't let anyone know it was you."

I watched her return to the lobby. I took the paper and noted that the burial was the next day at noon. "I need to take a long walk," I told Joanne and watched her disappear as the elevator doors closed.

When I returned, the office was empty and sunset was turning the cityscape orange. I turned on the wall of TVs and poured three fingers of Jack Daniels over ice. With my feet up on the black leather ottoman, relaxing my head on the back of the couch, I dozed off from emotional exhaustion. The night-lights shining through the panoramic cityscape woke me. I started to undress, walking into the office hotel suite and shut the door, tossing my boxers onto the bathroom floor. I walked into the shower. Closing my eyes, I let the hot spray of water wash away the pain of seeing *Nava snatching the business card from my hand.*

Startled, I felt a touch. I turned and saw Joanne running her hands over my shoulders. Her tight, toned, naked body still showed the bruises from our Tunis mission. Hypnotized by her long black hair and those clear blue eyes, she pressed into me, causing me to quiver. I started to say something when she put her long index finger to my lips. "Aponi told me there would be times when a Comanche warrior should not be alone. I think this is one of those times."

The shower was steaming. Joanne's intense blue eyes burned through me. She tossed her wet black hair wildly; her body pounded against me. The intensity was emancipating.

The next morning Joanne sat at the front desk and handed me the paper opened to Nava's picture, "Today is for her," she said.

I stared at it and then folded the New York Times, placing it under my arm, and walked to 7th Avenue. I was curious if the store would be open on the day of Nava's funeral.

The closer I got, the more anxious I became. The sky became darker as it began to drizzle. Approaching the storefront, my heart started to pound. I looked through the storefront. Someone other than Velvel was inside. *He must be at the funeral.* My heart relaxed and I felt a sense of relief. I walked a block thinking, *I need to make sure.* I turned and walked back to the store. The doorbell jingled as I entered.

"May I help you?" a voice asked. It was a man I didn't recognize. "I came here a few months ago looking for a gift," I said.

"Ah, I'm Yari. I'm new here. You must have talked to the owner, Velvel."

"Yes. Yes, that's correct." *Thinking he would tell me he's not in today.*

Then Yari said, "He just stepped out to get coffee and bagels. He should be back soon."

Not what I wanted to hear. I gave Yari an emotionless stare. "Sir, are you alright?" Yari's voice became nervous.

"Thanks. I'll wait." I browsed, but everywhere I looked I saw Nava's face. The tiny bell jingled when the door opened. Velvel had two coffees and a bag of bagels in hand.

Yari pointed and said, "Velvel, that gentleman is here to see you."

Velvel was surprised. "Ah, Mr. Toscano. I am so pleased. Let me put these down." He walked to the back to put his coffees and bagels on a small desk he used as a kitchen table. Yari skipped in to retrieve his breakfast.

I walked to the counter. Velvel met me standing behind it and smiled, sporting garlic and onion schmear on both corners of his mouth. "Mr. Toscano, how is your beautiful wife?" Velvel asked. I was too angry to respond. Velvel glanced at Yari, drinking his coffee. "Yari, this is Aponi's husband, Kachada Toscano," he said trying to break the uncomfortable silence.

Yari took a moment away from his java. "Ah, what kind of name is Kachada if I may ask?"

"It's Comanche," I replied. I gave Velvel a cold stare, making both Yari and Velvel more nervous.

Then I said, "Velvel, I am not here to talk about Aponi. I am here to ask you about this." I carefully unfolded the *New York Times*, revealing Nava's picture, and gently pushed the paper toward him. The only sound was the buzzing of the neon "open" sign hanging in the storefront window. Velvel's face turned whiter than the schmear on his face.

Without taking his nervous eyes off me, Velvel said, "This must be the bastard who gave Nava the phone number." Speaking to Yari in Yiddish.

Yari replied in Yiddish, "That whore bitch."

"Whore bitch?" I said in Yiddish.

They both were startled and began twitching after hearing me speak their tongue. Drops of perspiration began to drip from Velvel's forehead. "Very sad," he said, staring at Nava's picture.

I grabbed him by his two peyots. In one violent motion, I pulled him towards me, smashing his face through the cheap glass countertop. The sound of breaking glass slicing his face camouflaged the sound of ripping flesh and his screams. Both my right and left hands held Velvel's peyots. Blood was spilling from both sides of his head. Yari dropped his coffee and ran like he had shit in his pants. I dashed to my right and took the fool by the back of his wrinkled shirt, and tossed him into the wall, then lifted him a foot off the floor.

I repeated what he said in Yiddish, "Whore bitch." His body was limp from fear. I took a small black circular display pedestal from the counter and showed him no mercy. I shoved it into his mouth. Blood and broken teeth dribbled from his mouth as I dropped him onto the floor. Velvel sat on the floor with his back against the wall, shaking, unable to move.

I kneeled next to Velvel and whispered in his ear, "When you look in the mirror, I want you to remember Nava." I reached into my jacket pocket and took out my Swiss army knife and opened it. I took a handful of dirty hair on his head, looking into his eyes, and cut off his right ear. He opened his mouth, exposing his tonsils with a piercing scream. I took the bloody severed ear and neatly place it into his shirt pocket as a souvenir. Then I wiped my hands and knife on his bloodstained shirt and stood up staring down at him.

I walked to the sink to wash the blood from my hands. I returned seeing Yari sitting in his own urine and shit-stained pants. Velvel was shivering in the corner, holding his head where his ear once was. I picked up his black bowl hat from the floor and put it on my head. Velvel's eyes followed me as his body shook. As I was leaving I remembered the bagels in the kitchen, I walked past Yari and put the remaining schmear and bagels in the brown bag. Before I left I turned off the open sign, killing the buzzing sound, and closed the door.

"You were right Mr. Toscano. I have changed my mind about you," said Senator Rubin.

"I knew you would Senator," I said.

I couldn't bring Nava back, but I did make sure her death was a constant reminder that

Velvel would live with for the rest of his life. Every time Velvel looked into the mirror, he would see his deformed head, and think of Nava. On my way to the office, a street musician was playing the saxophone. I set the bowl hat down and placed the bag of bagels and schmear into the hat. The drizzling rain stopped and I looked up as the sun broke through the clouds. I continued on, listening to the musician play, "When The Saints Go Marching In."

CHAPTER 22

June 25, 1976,
Langley, Virginia

Director Panos and Zane were having a heated discussion in the conference room when Joanne and I arrived at Langley for a briefing.

"Kachada, Joanne, glad to see you again. Kachada, your family, are they doing well?" Director Panos asked.

"Yes. And thank you again for helping us during that Atlanta incident," I said.

The director said, "We protect our people." I noticed him giving Zane a quick look I found unnerving.

Zane took over and said, "Our target is not where we expected him to be."

"You mean Nisar?" asked Joanne.

"Yes. Nisar Uzza," Zane confirmed.

"What about Abu?" I inquired. Zane shook his head no.

Director Panos then got up and said his goodbyes, leaving Joanne, and me with Zane. Max stood outside the soundproof room. No one could come in or leave without his approval.

Joanne demanded, "So where is he, Zane?"

Zane gave us his serious face. "Are you ready for this one?" he said. Joanne and I shrugged. Zane grinned, "He's in Disney World," Zane chuckled. "Surprise."

"Disney World," Joanne scoffed. "What the *fuck*."

Zane pulled out an eight-by-ten photo of a Latin woman, about thirty years old. "Meet Maria. She works for us. She recognized him checking into the Polynesian Village Resort."

"How did he pass through the airport security?" Joanne asked.

"He posed as Phillippe Essifi, President of Investments with Essifi Club Resorts. He said he was visiting Disney World to open a theme park in France. The connection is the Essifi Club Resort in Tunisia. We have no idea how he got into the country without being seen by the FBI," Zane said.

"Tunisia," Joanne said with a biting tone.

"Yes, I know how you feel. He was somewhere in Tunis when we attacked the compound." Zane replied.

"Bastard," Joanne muttered.

"How does Essifi Club Resorts play into this?" I asked.

Zane explained, "They invested radical money into the project. The idea was to funnel money to Nisar and Abu's terrorist groups."

"So he wasn't staying at the compound. Our precious Intel was wrong," Joanne snapped.

"We don't know if he was there when we attacked. He could have arrived later," Zane replied.

"Our intelligence was still wrong. We risked our lives for what? A few misguided disciples?" Joanne asked.

Zane, frustrated said, "It's over. Let's move on." Joanne gave Zane her fuck-you look.

Zane went on with the briefing, "Okay, here's the plan: Phillippe Essifi, a.k.a. Nisar Uzza. As I mentioned, he is staying at the Polynesian Village Resort. His room is on the top floor overlooking the Lava Pools and the Polynesian Beach. He has four rooms, taking up the entire Lava Pool view from the back. He's traveling with his third wife, two kids that are seven and ten years old. But he's spending most of his time with his companions."

Joanne, still annoyed, asked, "Companions?"

Zane managed a subtle laugh, "Yes, they are escorts delivered from an international escort service for this trip. Nisar has a notorious reputation for traveling with estranged women."

Joanne spits out, "Fucking pig."

Zane cut in, "You two are going to check in to one of the Village Bungalows on the water directly across from his room's view."

"Just the two of us? Together?" Joanne asked.

Zane said. "Yes, you and Kachada are checking in as Mr. and Mrs. John Carter from Atlanta. You're newlyweds." I shrugged my shoulders. Zane continued, "I'll check into one of the Polynesian Village Villas as a traveling computer nerd working for BP under the name Brian Ouer."

I asked, "Silly question, but is Disney aware of this?"

Zane said, "No. So we will not bring any weapons with us. They will be in our rooms when we arrive. Our goal is to take him out without anyone the wiser."

"If they don't know about this, then how do you get our weapons in the room?" Joanne asked.

"Just know they will be there," Zane said. "Sirhan and Amid are Nisar's two bodyguards he travels with. One of them is always with him."

I asked, "How do we make the connection?"

"Nisar—or rather, Philippe—can't keep his eyes off attractive women." He turned to Joanne. "Enter Joanne. You are going to be our bait," Zane said.

Joanne irritated. "Bait?"

"From our research," Zane said, "you fit the profile Nisar is attracted to. He has a hard-on for attractive younger Middle Eastern women. You're a match. We're certain he'll take the bait."

Joanne says, "So now I'm no more than a worm on a hook."

Zane pulled out pictures of clothes and accessories, ignoring her comment. "You'll have a poolside wardrobe we believe will lure him. The idea is to get him to make contact with you once he sees you poolside. When he does, your job is to find out his schedule. Then we decide where and how we take him out. Naturally, doing our best to keep others in the park out of danger."

Joanne looked at the images. "So I'm supposed to basically walk around naked?"

"If you're uncomfortable?" Zane asked.

Joanne interrupted, "I will do whatever it takes to kill that pig." Then she looked towards me and said, "Besides, I've been seen in less."

Zane caught the vibe. "Well, we 're scheduled to check in Friday evening, July 23, booked through July 30, the following Friday." Zane reviewed his notes. "Nisar and his family are booked through Sunday, August 1. Our goal is to find a way to get to him before he leaves the park."

"So my job is to catch his interest and find out where he's going throughout the park?" Joanne asked.

"Yes," Zane said. "We know he's fascinated by the Pirates of the Caribbean, Animal Kingdom, and the Magic Kingdom." Zane went on, "We check in on July 23 and make contact at the patio in Trader Sam's. That will be our meeting place."

I asked, "What if we don't find an opening? What then?"

Zane replied, "We reluctantly let him enjoy his stay and wait for another opportunity,"

I asked, "How long have you been tracking him?"

"Since 1969. Seven years," Zane said.

Joanne gave a sharp response, "We take him at Disney."

Zane paused. "We must find a way to do so without putting anyone else in danger," Zane said. "We'll fly you back to the city. Your reservations for the airline and parking pass will be sent to you by tomorrow. I'll make contact when you arrive."

"Hello. We have reservations. Mr. and Mrs. John Carter."

The hotel receptionist asked, "Your driver's license and credit card, please." I handed them over.

The receptionist said, "Yes, Joanne and John. Welcome to the Disney's Polynesian Village Resort, Mr. and Mrs. Carter. Here are your license and card back and your hotel key cards. Our bellman will take your luggage to your Village Bungalow. Please follow him to Bungalow 10. It's one of our favorites among the honeymooners. You'll love it. Enjoy your stay, and please don't hesitate to call us if you need anything."

As we were leaving, the receptionist called out, "Ah, wait. You have a package waiting for you in your bungalow. My records show the package arrived earlier today." She smiled. "And congratulations. You two make such a beautiful couple."

Joanne put her arm around me, smiled and said, "Yes, we do."

Once in the bungalow, I shut the door and turned to the package sitting on the bed. Joanne opened a wooden box the size of a microwave and pulled out two Desert Eagles with silencers, and eight clips of bullets. "They must think we're going to shoot the place up," Joanne said.

I opened the sliding wood louvered doors and walked onto our private dock overlooking the Lava Pool and the sandy beach where I spotted two smaller swimming pools and a hot tub. Joanne relaxed and took off her top.

She lay on the bed in her sheer bra, white shorts, and sandals with clear painted toes nails. The phone rang.

Joanne answered. "Hello, Brian? Yes. Ten minutes?" She hung up, put her blouse on and said, "Zane, a.k.a. Brian will meet us at Trader Sam's in ten minutes."

We put our weapons in the room safe and left dressed as typical Disney World visitors. White shorts, cotton t-shirts—Joanne wearing a light powder blue and me in black—with sandals and sunglasses, to blend in.

"What a handsome couple," Zane chirped, sitting at the patio bar holding an umbrella drink.

Joanne replied, "That's the idea, Brian."

"I ordered a Mickey with rum for Mister and a Minnie with gin for the Misses," Zane said. We sipped on the mouse-eared umbrella drinks, knowing we were there to turn Disney's slogan "America on Parade" celebrating America's the two hundred years after the signing of the Declaration of Independence into our celebration of freeing the world from the likes of Nisar, a.k.a. Phillippe.

"Langley had your sizes on file. Does everything fit?" Zane asked.

Joanne winked. "Not much there to worry about. What else does Langley have I should know about?"

"Perfect," Zane said, ignoring Joanne's question. "I'm sure Nisar will appreciate the selection."

"What happens if he takes Joanne someplace out of sight? Like his room?" I asked.

"Joanne makes the call if she's comfortable or not. The whole idea is to lure him in to talk to her. Hopefully, you can find out where he's going and what time. From there we'll determine the best way to move forward." Zane put down his drink and said, "Now, I'm going to enjoy a few rides at the park myself. Talk later."

Joanne turned to me and asked, "Have a favorite ride?"

"Space Mountain."

Joanne smiled. "Good answer."

Joanne was ready to take in the early morning rays. Her flawless skin showed every muscle of her perfectly proportioned frame. The only accessories needed for her chic black string bikini was the right bling—a silver necklace with small white pearls, diamond earrings, a diamond-studded wristwatch, and a simple sexy silver toe ring. I watched as she tied her long black hair into a ponytail, finishing it off with a pair of Hollywood sunglasses. She dropped a gauzy black crop top into her black leather designer bag and made her exit.

I waited ten minutes before I joined her in my black swim shorts, black muscle tee, and black John Lennon-style sunglasses. I had pulled my hair into a man-tail. Our objective was to give the appearance of a wealthy young narcissistic couple that thought they had the world by the balls.

Joanne placed our lounge chairs on the beach in clear view of Nisar's balcony. I took a dip and relaxed on the hotel beach towel. My character was to barely notice Joanne and act the part of a rich arrogant husband ignoring his bride. Together we lay, baking side-by-side on our chaise lounges, until high noon. No Nisar. We gathered our things returned to our bungalow. We showered and rode a few more park rides.

Joanne and I replayed her beachside routine Sunday and Monday, with no Nisar in sight. Again after a long afternoon in the sun, Joanne once again retreated to our bungalow.

"We only have three days left. If all else fails we have to take him in his room," Joanne said.

"That means whoever gets in our way becomes a victim," I said with regret.

"I know. But we can't let him leave here alive," Joanne insisted.

I said, "We still two more days."

The next morning Joanne was coming out of the beach water, strutting to her chaise lounge shaking out her thick black hair. She moved her routine to the Lava Pool area hoping to be more visible and took on an innocent yet provocative position with hopes of luring Nisar to the pool. She moved from one sexy exhibition to another while I made my entrance as the self-centered husband. Nisar's girls had arrived at the pool and set up close to Joanne. I spoke loud enough so they could hear me, "I'm going to the park. You can soak up sun while I enjoy the rides." I left Joanne alone hoping Nisar might join his escorts at the pool.

"Asshole," Joanne barked.

I returned to the bungalow, peeking through shutters. I watched Nisar's exotic harem make their way over to Joanne. One offered to lotion her back. Joanne politely refused and turned over as the girls jumped back into the pool. There was still no sign of Nisar and it was closing in on 2:00 p.m. I started to believe Nisar was not interested.

Finally—voila! Our target, Nisar, arrived to join his two escorts. It was the first time we had put eyes on the man responsible for so many horrific crimes. His thick black hair was wet and combed straight back, his beard was trimmed into a Van Dyke, groomed tightly to his face. He was much taller than I expected, not the fat slob presented to us by the CIA's dossier. The tall, dark, and handsome man with pearly white teeth looked as if he had walked out of a 1950s Rock Hudson poster. If you didn't know any better, you would have thought he was quite a catch.

Joanne reclined onto her lounge, turning over and providing a more provocative image, untying her top, leaving a view of her tight behind. Her yummy invitation caught the attention of Nisar's escorts. Nisar followed their eyes to Joanne. Joanne then turned over to let her nipples play peek-a-boo with her top, a new addition to her routine.

Nisar became fixated on her, and his manhood gained the attention of his two escorts, who fondly approved. They giggled and jumped into the pool, pulling Nisar into the water to get him closer to them. They bounced around in the water, taking turns wrapping their legs around him. To a normal pair of eyes, Nisar appeared to be a fun-loving playboy. He took off his shirt and tossed it onto a chaise lounge from the water, showing off his expensive solid gold chain necklace nestled into his hairy chest. He sneaked a glance at Joanne to see if she noticed him.

Joanne nonchalantly got up and gathered her things. She slipped on her thin black t-shirt. With one quick flick of her wrist, she took off the tiny bikini top from beneath her shirt. The transparent shirt outlined her nipples as she strutted to the bungalow followed by Nisar's eyes. She now had his attention.

Joanne walked in and said, "Finally."

"He liked what he saw," I remarked. Then I told her, "Zane has a table reserved at the 'Ohana thirty minutes from now."

Joanne walked away saying, "I only need ten."

"If you need help just let me know," I said teasing her.

Joanne says, "Disney calls it, 'America on Parade." Joanne stares, "Well, it takes more than one to make a parade," and takes off her top then struts into the shower.

CHAPTER 23

July 28, 1976, Disney World

An hour passed and still no Nisar. Joanne was on the chaise lounge in her hot pink string bikini. From the bungalow, out of eyeshot, I waited, watching for any signs of Nisar. After thirty minutes, I began to worry. Part of me didn't want Nisar to show. I tried to remind myself Joanne had been trained by Mossad. Just then Nisar arrived.

I dialed Zane. "He's arrived." I continued to feed Zane the action as it unfolded. "Mrs. Carter moved closer to Nisar dipping into the pool. She's doing her shake-out-my-hair routine at her chaise lounge. Nisar has started a conversation."

Zane said, "I'm going to get a closer look." He hung up.

Nisar had the waiter deliver Joanne a drink. She sat up, letting the untied top slip, revealing enough to tease Nisar, and put her sunglasses on. *If only I could hear them.* She took a sip and Nisar moved his chaise lounge next to her, staring at Joanne like a hungry panther ready to pounce.

The phone rang. "Could you hear them?" I asked Zane.

Zane said, "I couldn't make out what they were saying. But I saw him move closer."

"She's touching his arm," I shouted.

"You need to chill and let her do her job," Zane said and hung up.

I watched like a peeping tom as she looked down at her expensive diamond watch. Nisar leaned close and puts his hand her leg. She smiled and stood up, teasing him with a view of her tiny ass. Nisar reached out to her. She took his hand and says something. *Damn, I hate not hearing them.* She turned, showing off her sexy strut towards our bungalow.

Joanne was excited when she entered. "He's mine," she said. She flashed me a glance and ordered me to call Zane so she could download both of us. It was only five minutes till Zane arrived.

"Nisar asked if I would join him on the Jungle Cruise tomorrow," Joanne said.

Zane was excited. "Great job. Sounds like our plan is working."

I spoke up, "Do we really try to take him out on one of the rides?"

Joanne interjected, "Too dangerous. We should take him out in his room."

"That may be the best way," Zane said and turned to Joanne. "Are you comfortable doing that? It could be dangerous."

Joanne was determined and said, "I can take care of myself. I think it's the only way."

Not happy about this I said, "I hate seeing you put in that position."

Zane acknowledged my concern, "Kachada is right, Joanne, you need to be careful."

Joanne fired back, "I'll be fine. Besides, I have both of you for backup."

"What about his bodyguards?" I asked. "What if they are in the room?"

"No way for us to know," said Zane. "We agreed before we came here that the target was worth the risk."

Joanne said, "I'm not leaving here until he's dead."

Zane reminded us, "We need to understand we could find ourselves in a situation where the family gets caught in the middle." Zane went on, "Anyone standing in that room when we enter cannot be left alive. Understood?"

Joanne grit her teeth. "Yeah. I get it. I pray the family is nowhere near that room."

"I'm going to walk the beach area for a better idea of what's around," I said.

"I should go with you to keep a husband-wife thing going," Joanne suggested.

"Good idea. Nisar could be watching you. You know this guy—it will make him lust even more seeing you with your ungrateful husband," Zane said. "All he cares about right now is conquering you."

Joanne took my arm and said, "Let's give that pig a show."

We walked to the dock overlooking the beach hand in hand, snuggling and stopping to kiss every so often. On our stroll I discovered a small work shed.

Joanne was flustered. "What are you doing?" she asked.

"I want to see what's inside." I opened the door, revealing landscape shovels, bags of sand, and rakes.

"This place is too perfect. Even their yard tools are neatly arranged." She snickered. "I can see him watching us from his balcony," Joanne said.

I stopped and gave her a long, passionate kiss. "Mm, that was a nice surprise," Joanne admitted.

"I worry about you being alone with him. I don't want you to become a sacrifice in this operation just to kill him," I said.

"I won't—and if I do," she insisted, "you better do what is necessary." She left and returned to the bungalow while I walked alone, to remind Nisar that I didn't appreciate my beautiful bride.

Suddenly I saw Zane run into a nearby building. Curious, I followed him. It was an employee locker room where the Mickey Mouse costumes were kept. He was talking to one of the actors. I surprised him when I asked, "You freelancing now?"

Zane just ignored me and kept talking to the employee. "Here's a grand, and you get another when I return it." He turned to me and asked, "Are you following me?"

"I saw you walk in here so I was curious," I said.

The young actor returned with a Mickey Mouse costume and said, "They won't miss it; we have a whole rack of them like those hanging over there." He pointed to the rack of Mickey Mouse costumes, with the large Mickey heads lined up in a row above them, and said, "I hope the prank works and your boss is surprised."

Zane said sarcastically, "Oh, believe me, he will be. Thanks. Oh—is there a pocket in this costume?"

"Yes, two," the young man said and pulled out both pants pockets.

Zane was amused. "Wow, those are huge." He introduced me to the employee. "Mr. Carter works with me and is in on our little prank."

The young actor enjoyed the attention. "Hey, cool. Yes—we carry all kind of toys, tickets, and pamphlets to sign and hand out to kids," he said.

Zane asked, "Do you think I could use a couple to make it more fun?"

"Sure—and here, take an oversized pen. That always gets a smile," the young man said.

"Hey, thanks. That's perfect," Zane told him.

The employee said, "Thank you—I can use the money." He held up a pair of oversized red floppy shoes. "Don't forget these."

Zane waved off the idea. "No, I'll wear sneakers. I'll just end up tripping over those big boys and ruin the surprise." The actor left and Zane said, "So, what do you think?"

I gave him my wise guy answer, "About you moonlighting as Mickey Mouse?"

Annoyed, Zane replied, "No asshole. This is how I'm going to get into the apartment next to Nisar."

I laughed. "Really?"

Zane snapped, "In this costume, I can go anywhere and no one will question me. We need to get in position to get to Nisar quickly. With this I can get into the apartment next door."

"Where am I while this is going on?" I asked.

"You're watching from your bungalow. When she leaves with him, you head to the back stairs and make your way up to the fourth floor. His room is the last one by the stairway. Joanne will be between you and me. That way we can reach her within seconds."

"That actually sounds like a smart idea," I admitted.

"And to think, you're the one with a brilliant mind. Let me get this to my room while you parade around the beach like a young cock," Zane barked.

"Sure thing, Mick," I chuckled.

"Fuck you," Zane sneered. He walked away with the oversized costume hanging out of his duffle bag.

I continued to scout the area and noticed a golf cart with a young maintenance woman riding by. There were several sizeable blue canvas laundry bags tied to the back of it. I followed her to the side of the hotel where three carts were being unloaded. I walked up and asked, "Wow! Is this all laundry?"

Surprised, she said, "Yes sir; it's just one of the hundreds of bags we bring in every day. You're not supposed to be here, sir."

I avoided her comment. "You do this every day?"

"Four times a day. A lot of rooms means a lot of laundry—and some people, well, they know how to make a mess," she said.

"I guess so. I promise I won't be one of them," I said.

"Oh, don't worry. Just enjoy your stay and let us worry about that, sir." She was Disney polite.

I walked away noticing a giant alligator sitting on the small beach across from us.

"Hey," I called out to the employee pointing. "There's a gator on the beach over there!"

"Yeah, we call him Gordo. He's a regular," the employee said.

"A regular. Isn't that dangerous?" I asked her.

She said with a laugh. "Only if you try to pet him. That's why the sign says *"No Swimming. There are gators in this area."*

"Thanks," I said and returned to the bungalow.

Joanne was sipping a gin and tonic with her feet up on dock railing with the sliding doors open when I arrived. "I can see Nisar spying on me," she said wearing white shorts that were just long enough and her braless sheer white cotton top. "He's been watching me since I sat here."

I leaned down to her and whispered, "We should make him jealous." I picked her up, nuzzled her breast, and carried her off. She giggled. "Hey, I didn't expect that."

"I wanted to play the newlywed game for him," I said and put her on the bed, then walked back to the dock.

"Do you think he can see into the room?" Joanne asked.

I looked straight ahead while trying to glance over to his balcony area. "Maybe."

"We should finish what you started," she said, and in one motion took off her blouse and slid her tight white shorts down, revealing her Brazilian trim. My heart pounded. *I thought back to the wild beast in the shower.* I walked to the bedside leaving the sliding doors open to the dock and joined her. She whispered, "Now I know how you must feel."

Confused, I asked, "What do you mean?"

Her bright blue eyes connected with mine and pulled me to her. "Counting the minutes," she whispered. "Make me forget about tomorrow," she said after engulfing me with her legs.

I attached the silencer to my Desert Eagle and covered it with my long black tee shirt. The baggy shirt hid the silhouette of the gun and two clips. I watched Joanne put on her tiny white bikini. Sitting on the edge of the bed, I asked, "How are you going to protect yourself? There's no place to hide a weapon."

Joanne leaped like a panther, throwing her muscular thighs around my neck, squeezing as she sat on top of me. I began to cough and pass out from the power of her thigh muscles. She loosened her grip and slid to my side. "That's one of my many weapons," she said.

I struggled to catch my breath, my voice hoarse, coughing.

"I'm not afraid," she said, then gave me a quick kiss, and walked to the beach.

I rubbed my neck, trying to get my voice back, and went to the dock area. I took a sip of water, trying to loosen my throat. When she arrived at Lava Pool, she relaxed into the chaise lounge—going into her well-rehearsed sunning and dipping routine.

I noticed Zane walking towards the main lobby of the Polynesian Village. He was wearing the Mickey costume. A group of children was in front of the lobby attacking him. He played the role of a pro, signing autographs and taking pictures with the kids and their parents.

"Oh shit." Another Mickey Mouse was running to Zane with his huge feet flopping. They began to argue. The mouse made the mistake of putting one of this three fat mouse fingers in Zane's chest. Zane took one of his oversized mouse ears and twisted his head, knocking him to the ground. It was a mouse fight right in front of the kids and parents.

The other mouse managed to get up and run away, flopping his yellow feet as fast as they could carry him. The children were laughing and cheering Zane. The parents looked shocked as Zane signed more autographs, giving them high fives, then he went into the lobby. I couldn't believe that had happened. The levity of it was a welcomed distraction from what we are about to do.

I turned my attention to Joanne relaxing on the chaise lounge. She was unaware of the Mickey Mouse fight. Nisar had made his appearance. He was standing tall, looking around the pool area as if he knew he was being watched. For a moment I thought the gig was up. He continued toward Joanne and sat on the chaise lounge, moving it right next to her. She smiled as they began talking.

I held the brick cell phone and dialed Zane. "Minnie is making contact with Goofy," I said.

"What's with this Minnie and Goofy shit?" Asked Zane.

"I thought it was appropriate, considering where we are," I said.

Zane said, "Whatever. Kachada, I'm inside making my way to the fourth floor."

"I saw the mouse fight," I interjected.

"Can you believe that mouse? He screamed I was working his area, that mouse fuck. You should be headed this way," Zane said.

"How do you know the family isn't there?" I asked.

"I saw them leaving earlier with Sirhan, one of Nisar's bodyguards. They should be gone for the day," Zane said.

"I hope so," I said.

Zane commanded, "Like we discussed, if there is a guard out in front of his room,

I'll take him out. Then you follow me into the room. We attack without any concern for anyone around us. It needs to be quick and quiet as possible."

I noticed Joanne leaving with Nisar and said, "Joanne is going into the lobby with Nisar."

"I see them. You should start heading this way," Zane said.

I left the bungalow to make a stop at the landscaping shed and laundry dispatch. Then I continued to the maintenance elevator to the fourth floor. My stomach was queasy as I arrived in the hallway and watched the reflections in the floor-to-ceiling hallway windows. Amid walked out of Nisar's suite and stood by the door. This meant Nisar was making his move alone with Joanne. Amid was a thick man, about six feet six inches tall, with brown skin, a broad body, and no hair on his head. We would have to go through him to get to Nisar.

Just then Zane came around the corner in his Mickey costume, waving to Amid. "Mickey," Amid said in broken English like a kid.

Zane walked up to Amid, who had taken on a childlike grin as Zane reached into his costume pocket. I freaked out. *Oh fuck, he's gonna shoot him.* I prepared to spring into action when Zane pulled out a picture and the oversized pen from his pockets. He signed it and handed Amid the photo and walked down the hall. I was still hyperventilating after that false alarm. Amid smiled from one muscled ear to the other. Zane ducked into the apartment next door while Amid was fixated on his souvenir. I remained still, calming myself down, as I watched the reflections in the windows. Everything appeared to be under control.

Then I heard, "No, I don't feel like it."

I jumped, surprised by the commotion coming from the elevator. *Shit.* Nisar's family was returning from the park. *Fuck.* The girl looked as though she was sick, and stopped to barf. They walked towards Nisar's suite. As they tried to go in Amid stopped them. They knew Nisar was not alone. Nisar's wife started shouting in Arabic, and chaos erupted in front of Nisar's suite.

Right behind them, two hotel security guards came running, following the other Mickey Mouse from the fight. He passed by Nisar's family, screaming, "That's the fake mouse. He threatened me." He pointed at Zane, standing inside by the open door of the suite next to Nisar's still wearing the mouse pants.

Zane had no choice but to attack the other Mickey, knocking him onto the floor with the handle of his Desert Eagle and charging toward Nisar's room. The security guards were surprised and froze long enough for Zane to make it into the room behind Amid. I was sick of the thought of what could happen to Joanne. I ran right behind him. Sirhan pushed the family to the floor and ran towards me. *"Fuck."* I turned before going in and shot Sirhan in the chest. I watched him fall to the floor and dashed into Nisar's room.

The other Mickey Mouse had shaken off the hit by Zane and ran into Nisar's suite. The sounds a succession of quick shots fired came from the hallway. Sirhan came into the room, bleeding from his chest, and violently struck the other Mickey on the back of the head, knocking him once again to the floor. He slammed the door shut.

I immediately put a bullet into Sirhan's head, blowing off half his face before he could shoot Zane. Blood splattered across the wall, carpet, and onto the bed. The family was in shock, on the floor screaming. Nisar's wife squeezed the two children to her.

Zane was covered in blood from my shooting of Sirhan. As Amid turned to protect Nisar, Zane put two rounds into his chest from the side, dropping him onto the bed. He fell onto Joanne, who sat on top of a naked Nisar with her legs around his throat. The force of Amid's body knocked her off Nisar and onto the floor. Nisar toppled on top of her. Zane put another bullet into Amid to make sure he wasn't going to be a problem.

Joanne threw her legs around Nisar's head again and tried to roll him toward the nightstand, squeezing his neck like she did mine. Nisar stretched for his Khanjar knife on the nightstand. Somehow, Amid managed to push Joanne over. I put the fourth shot into

Amid from the back. In all the chaos, Nisar managed to grab a handful of Joanne's hair, pulling her toward him. He put his knife to her throat. All of this happened in less than four minutes. The knife was so tight to Joanne's throat it was turning her perfect white skin red. Zane looked at me and I glanced back, then we turned our focus on Joanne. She was determined to get revenge for her family.

Nisar screamed in French, "I will slit her throat if you don't leave right now."

The other Mickey got back up, not realizing what he'd gotten himself into, and said "What the f . . ." I smacked him with the steel handle of my Desert Eagle, knocking him out one more time. In one swift move, I punched the mother and took the boy. At this moment, we were at a stalemate with Nisar's knife to Joanne's throat and my Pistol to his young son's head. We knew Nisar would do anything to save his son.

Amid surprised us all again when he stood up. Zane shot two more rounds into him. Zane then pointed his Desert Eagle at

Nisar's head. The young daughter screamed, clutching her mother's abaya *cloak*.

Zane spoke Hebrew, "If you don't let her go your family will die with you." If Nisar thought we were the Mossad, he knew then we would kill the entire family without hesitation if he didn't let Joanne go.

Nisar, holding Joanne's head by her hair, pushed his knife deeper into her throat, causing more blood to flow, screaming in Arabic, "I will kill this Jew bitch."

Nisar was hysterical. I locked onto Joanne's eyes as she did mine. She remained calm. Struggling to breathe, she mouthed the words, "You promised."

Zane again said in Hebrew, "Nisar, do you want to die knowing you killed your entire family?"

I lifted the boy off the ground by his shirt, pushing my Desert Eagle into the side of his head, knowing he was our only hope. Terrorized, Nisar squirmed. I Pushed my Desert Eagle into his ear I shouted, "I will start with him."

Nisar's eyes bounced from his son to Zane to me and back to his son, hyperventilating. I glanced over at Zane, and his eyes went straight to mine. I turned back to Joanne—all of this within less than fifteen seconds. I knew what was going to happen. Joanne's eyes meet mine, then she closed them, smiling and grabbed Nisar's hand, pushing his knife into her throat.

Losing my mind, I let out a Comanche war cry. Inside my head I saw *Comanche warriors brutally attacking the Pawnee village, leaving the ground slippery from the blood, as I heard Chief Nocona chanting, "Leave no enemy alive."*

"Kachada. Kachada." Zane was calling me. The boy was lying on the floor in a puddle of blood. At that moment I knew what I must have done. The suite was motionless with only the sounds of faint cries coming from Nisar. The savage scene was accentuated by the sweet smell of vanilla incense hovering over the room of bloody bodies.

On the floor next to the bed was Joanne's lifeless naked body. Her throat was bleeding from the blade of Nisar's knife. Zane stood as still as a stone, holding his Desert Eagle pointed at Nisar. Zane was terrified by the violent rage he had just witnessed. My hand still gripped my pistol.

Zane, shaken walked around the room, looking at the bodies of Amid, Sirhan, the mother, the boy, the girl, and Joanne. Nisar's eyes were wide open with shock from witnessing the brutal scene of his family lying in blood. I crawled next to Joanne and held her close to me. My body, arms, and hands covered with blood, mixing with hers. I realized then that I had been shot in my shoulder.

Zane said under his breath, "You killed them all." All I could do was rock, holding the lifeless body of Joanne. "Nisar is alive," Zane stammered. "You left Nisar alive."

Zane put his hand over the blood coming from my shoulder. "Sirhan shot you before I shot the rest of his face off. We need to get you to our doctor."

I gently put Joanne down thinking, *she gave her life to kill the beast that murdered her parents.* I picked up the knife from the floor. "He comes with me," I said. "I have a promise to keep."

Zane, caught up in horror of the room asked, *"What?"*

"He comes with me," I said.

Zane reluctantly stepped back knowing now was the time to challenge me. Nisar stared at his son lying in a pool of blood. He let out a father's scream.

I shouted, "Justice is waiting."

Nisar's foggy eyes wandered towards me. I took my fist and hit his jaw, knocking him out. I could feel the pain shoot through my shoulder. I dragged his naked body to the doorway.

Zane, watching, said, "Kachada, you can't leave any evidence."

I hoisted Nisar over my bleeding shoulder and stalked out of the room. Behind me, I heard Zane make a phone call to Director Panos.

My body was covered in Joanne's blood as I went out the back door of the hotel. I dropped the heavy Nisar onto the golf cart and drove to the secluded beach cove behind the villas.

I dumped naked Nisar out of the cart to the ground, still unconscious. I pounded sharp steel stakes from the gardening shed through his skin staking him to the ground. The pain from the stakes brought Nisar back and was horrified watching me slowly sliced a section of skin from his hairy chest. He tried moving but he couldn't. *Joanne's face haunted me.* Nisar's painful grunts brought me back.

I kneeled next to the killer, speaking Arabic. "You are going to die a savage death." I held the bloody strip of skin I'd sliced from his body up for him to see. He squirmed, horrified at the sight of the meaty strip dangling from my hand. I tossed it to the edge of the water. Gordo the alligator was on the beach, watching the bloody meat turn the water red. The spectator sprang across the beach into the water, slamming his eighty blades of teeth shut.

Nisar winced, frightened at the sight. I sat back on my haunches and watched him try to move while moaning. His face and mouth were covered with sand, cementing to the blood from the hot sun.

I tied his hands and feet with the rope I brought from the shed and then removed the metal stakes. Then I pulled Nisar towards the water's edge. Gordo's cold eyes watched. He subtly revealed his razor-sharp teeth with a slight smile. Nisar tried to scream, but he couldn't. I had stuffed a tennis ball into his mouth before I pushed him close to the water. Blood dripping from my shoulder, I took out my rosary, rubbing them and began to pray. I gave him one last look before my final push watching him float towards Gordo.

Gordo slid into the water and sat in the water about ten feet from Nisar. His cold black eyes popped above the water's surface. Nisar's eyes watched as Gordo slowly floated closer. Gordo circled Nisar and stopped. Their eyes met a foot apart. Nisar's was fixed on Gordo's. Gordo's fixed on Nisar's. In slow motion, Gordo opened his mouth, exposing those vicious shredding tools as if to tease Nisar. Nisar's eyes become as big and black as Gordo's. Nisar twitched his eyes towards me. Gordo was patient. He had the sweet taste of meat and wanted more. He waited as if to give Nisar time to flash through his beastly life. All of a sudden, slam, Gordo chomped down on Nisar's head tearing half the skin from his head, leaving Nisar's frightened eyes nestled in his meat-covered skull, looking my way trying to scream through the blood-stained tennis ball. Gordo circled him as if to give Nisar a final glimpse of my face. Nisar's eyes followed him. Gordo couldn't wait any longer and violently attacked, the sounds of powerful splashes amid the crunching from chomping down on his skull, one following the next, turning the faint muffled sounds of Nisar's screams into nothingness.

"Kachada, you need to go," Zane called out running up to the water's edge. "We need to clean this up."

I just stood still, watching my friend Gordo return to his favorite spot in the sun. He looked my way and I swear I saw him give me a smile. The strain of my violence showed in Zane's face. I handed him the knife and said, "I kept my promise. Now find Abu."

I left blood covered golf cart and walked back to my bungalow carrying the memories of Joanne and those young faces to haunt me.

I finish the scotch, watching the senators' horrified faces.

"I now know why these pages were blacked out," Senator Wyatt said.

"Senator, believe me. It only gets blacker."

End of Day One
18,759,480 minutes after.

AN EXCERPT FROM MY FOLLOW UP NOVEL

DAY TWO

From our favorite spot on Mount Pinchot, Aponi and Knoton sat by my side watching God paint another beautiful sunset. I gently rubbed my rosary, reminding me my Comanche and Sicilian ancestors were always with me. As I stare off into the sunset I confessed. "My soul is covered in blood."

"The blood of beasts," Aponi whispered into my ear.

The sounds of pounding hooves came to a rapid stop. Kele sat on his Painted Pinto. "They are here," Kele said.

I climbed onto my silver stallion and took one last look at Aponi holding Knoton's hand. "Every minute is a precious diamond when I spend it with you," I said.

"They are waiting," Kele reminded me.

I gave my heels to the stallion, and broke into a gallop. I left Aponi standing tall, holding Knoton's hand tightly. Their silhouettes disappeared on the horizon.

I brought my horse to a sudden stop. Kele, worried, urged, "Kachada, don't go."

I took my best friend from my leather vest pocket and I stole a sniff, then gave my stallion a kick. The horse broke into a sprint, leaving Kele behind as I cried out, "Leave no enemy alive."

Day one of my testimony was ugly. But day two will expose the senators to an even blacker world, including the ugly beasts that live among them.

Lightning Source UK Ltd.
Milton Keynes UK
UKHW040432240219
337804UK00002B/76/P